Neither of them pulled any punches.

"I'm sorry I took you to the sawdust palace. I didn't mean to be uncivilized, I was just angry. Childish. . . Anyway, I'm sorry. I'm mad at my situation and I took it out on you."

"The fact is that place is right up my alley. Ain't nothing wrong with a good night of cowboy music, and don't you roll those pretty blue eyes at me, princess. You give it a shot before you knock it." He cleared his throat. "So what is an MIS manager?" John asked innocently.

"An MIS manager is someone that reports to the vice president with data on all information systems infrastructure and its components."

"That's kind of vague. You want to help me out here?"

"I coordinate the equipment needs for all the departments. I help them decide which computer systems will work best and eliminate the ones that don't work well."

"Ahhh."

"And what is it you do, Mr. Savitch? You own a suit; I suppose that's a good sign." She leaned in, setting her elbow on the table.

"Do you always say whatever you're thinking?" He met her blue eyes with his own and challenged her. She looked away quickly. He loved that she said what she thought. It was refreshing. Stefani Willems had more in common with him than she thought. Neither of them pulled any punches.

"As a matter of fact, I do say what I'm thinking," she said with an apologetic tone. "No sense in playing games. It's dishonest and annoying as far as I'm concerned." She shrugged. "It's just the way I am. I don't want to offend you, but that house is very special to me and—and I want to live there."

He saw her eyes glisten with moisture. The sight of true sentiment brought out his most tender feelings. Glory, she was beautiful—and too busy with her agenda to ever notice.

KRISTIN BILLERBECK makes her home in the Silicon Valley with her engineering director husband, Bryed, and their three small boys. In addition to writing, Kristin enjoys painting, reading, and conversing with her online group. Visit Kristin on the web at www.getset.com/kristinbillerbeck

Books by Kristin Billerbeck

HEARTSONG PRESENTS
HP247—Strong as the Redwood
HP294—To Truly See
HP329—Meet My Sister, Tess

Don't miss out on any of our super romances. Write to us at the following address for information on our newest releases and club information.

Heartsong Presents Readers' Service
PO Box 719
Uhrichsville, OH 44683

The Landlord Takes a Bride

Kristin Billerbeck

Heartsong Presents

To my mother, Kay Compani, who is
a. alive,
b. kindhearted, and
c. fiercely loyal
(unlike many of the mothers in my books).
And to my aunt, Mary Bechtel, who is like a second mother.
A second *good* mother. Much love, Kristin

A note from the author:
I love to hear from my readers! You may correspond with me by writing:

Kristin Billerbeck
Author Relations
PO Box 719
Uhrichsville, OH 44683

ISBN 1-57748-935-7

THE LANDLORD TAKES A BRIDE

Cover illustration by Victoria Lisi and Julius.

PRINTED IN THE U.S.A.

one

Stefani Willems looked to the apricot orchards behind the new house. Only three trees remained now, but the ghosts of their lost companions danced in her memory. She shook her head to dislodge the thoughts. This was a day for rejoicing, not sadness. A new house in San Francisco's peninsula was nearly unheard of, but she'd struggled for the right and triumphed. "I did it," she said aloud to herself. "It's mine. They'll be so proud."

She breathed a huge, cleansing sigh. And dreamt of her new kitchen. She loved to cook gourmet meals for relaxation. *Where is that real estate agent? He's fifteen minutes late.*

George Daily, her real estate agent, pulled up with a screech in his European convertible. His comb-over hairstyle was in disarray from the wind and he raked his stubby fingers through it as he approached her. His nervous smile alarmed her, and she felt her heart beat faster. *Oh, please, Lord, no. Don't let anything go wrong with this deal. You know what this house means to me.*

"Stefani," George said grimly and she felt her head shake involuntarily.

Before he finished his sentence, an expensive-looking sport utility vehicle whirled into the driveway and stopped uncomfortably close to them. George and Stefani stood mesmerized by the tall, mysterious man in a cowboy hat who emerged. A cowboy hat in California. The shadow from his hat cast across his face, yet still the sea green of his eyes shone and met hers.

Throw this guy in with the deal, and I'll be set for life! He left her speechless. Everything about him exuded confidence. His dangerous stare pulled her in. She *knew* him. She'd never seen him before, but, inexplicably, she *knew* him. He aggressively reached over, grasped her hand, and shook it. Stefani felt a bolt of electricity rush up her arm.

She released his hand as though it were a hot iron.

"You must be Kate," he said in a deep, rich baritone. "This here's perfect. Just like we talked about."

She shook her head to correct him, but nothing happened. She still hadn't found her voice. She was still lost in the magnificent green of his eyes.

After a long, awkward silence George finally intervened. "Mr. Savitch?" The rugged man nodded affirmatively. "This is Stefani Willems." George then turned to her and quietly added, "Mr. Savitch also put in a bid on the house. His was accepted."

Stefani felt her breath leave her. She looked to George for further explanation, but he conveniently avoided her gaze. Her perfect house: the right neighborhood, the separate rental unit for help with the mortgage, and, most of all, that heavenly, gourmet kitchen. Gone. *Gone! Swiped away by that gorgeous hunk of a man who would probably never use the kitchen. Not unless one of his harem can cook*, she thought viciously.

The stranger spoke, interrupting Stefani's dark thoughts. "I'm sorry, Miss Willems. I haven't seen the place, but if you like it, there must be something to it." He tipped his hat as if that made up for his stealing her house. A lopsided grin emerged and Stefani felt herself perused. His sea-green eyes lingered on her legs for just a moment too long and her anger built. If steam could have erupted from her ears, it would have. *Male chauvinist! To think I thought him handsome!* She chastised herself for being so shallow. Looks were fleeting. Didn't her grandmother always tell her that?

It was then she found her tongue. "You bought a house you've never seen?" she asked incredulously. His apologetic tone was wasted, his sympathy squandered. She could tell from his striking appearance that he was used to getting what he wanted. And right now, he obviously wanted to make her feel better about losing her dream house. *Impossible. An impossible feat.*

The cowboy continued. "I came from Colorado. I had to buy on faith so I'd have a place when I got here." He smiled that infuriating grin again and Stefani's jaw clenched. Didn't this guy know that he'd just stolen the one material possession she'd ever cared about? He kept on talking his charming sweet talk, oblivious to her rising temper. "My agent said housing is quite difficult to find around here, especially a new development, what with land being so scarce." He had no idea just how scarce *this* land was. "Kate assured me this was the best neighborhood. I'd say I was right lucky to get this investment." He clicked his tongue, blatantly pleased with himself. His words only infuriated Stefani further.

"It's more than an investment, Mr. Savitch," she blustered. "This home is equipped with a gourmet stove in each unit, wood shutters, and a whirlpool bathtub in each master bathroom. It's a home designed for someone who can appreciate its superior qualities, not as an *investment*." Stefani felt like her child had just been offended.

"Well, I reckon it's all that, too, Miss Willems." He crossed his brawny arms and looked at the house casually, with a shrug. "So you have a key?" he asked George. "Let's see the place."

George fumbled with the real estate lock and Stefani followed in unwittingly, holding back her tears as she stepped onto the hand-laid Mexican tile floor she had selected. During the planning stages, she had befriended the builder and expressly asked for the special flesh-toned tile for the entryway. The sight of it now made her wince.

She watched the new buyer as he walked through the house. He judged all the options *she'd* selected. He opened every cabinet and checked each tiny flaw in the paint. It gave her hope. "What's the matter? Not what you'd thought it would be? You can always withdraw your offer, you're not in escrow yet." She smiled a counterfeit smile and he looked at her with his brows furrowed. "This house doesn't seem to suit your tastes, anyway. Perhaps your agent might find you something more suitable."

"What's so special about this house, Miss Willems?"

"So you remember my name," she said coolly. "It's not something I can easily explain, but this property means a great deal to me."

"Is that so?" he replied evenly.

"Stefani, I think it's time we left Mr. Savitch alone in his new house." George grabbed her gently by the elbow, but she pulled away.

"I'm sure Mr. Savitch doesn't mind our being here, do you, Mr. Savitch?" She squared her shoulders and stared straight into those deep green eyes. No easy task. He had to be completely aware of his effect on women, and Stefani was determined she'd wouldn't fall victim to his charms. Superficial as they were. As her breathing quickened, she realized how difficult that might be. There was something so unnerving about people in real life that looked this good. They belonged on the movie screen or in the pages of a magazine, not here in real life.

Mr. Savitch gently lifted her arm onto his own and Stefani shuddered that his touch affected her. "I don't mind at all, Miss Willems. Why don't you give me the grand tour?"

He looked down upon her from his perch. She guessed him to be over six feet tall, but with that ridiculous cowboy hat. . . At five-six, Stefani was fairly tall, but this man made her feel small in every sense of the word. She broke free and purposely walked him into the living room. She was reminded where each piece of her furniture would have gone. She wondered if he even *had* any furniture.

He wasn't married, she could tell. Not just because he was void of a ring, but because he didn't dress as if any woman had a part in selecting his wardrobe. Too masculine. Add to that the fact that he'd hired a female real estate agent, and he *had* to be single.

She inhaled deeply. "Crown molding throughout. You don't see that kind of workmanship in California too often." She pointed to the ceiling line, while he watched her curiously. "The builder is into details."

"Uh-huh, nice," he said absently, though she noticed his eyes never left her and his arms remained crossed as he studied her.

She turned on her heel and leered at him, furious that he could be so indifferent about something that was so important to her. "Mr. Savitch, it's obvious you don't care about this house!" she accused. "Why don't you find something else? Something that suits your *bachelor* needs better. You know, maybe something where your stuffed animal heads might be more at home."

"Stefani!" George gasped. But Mr. Savitch only broke into a loud laugh, throwing his head back in sincere mirth.

"Miss Willems, I appreciate your concern about my *bachelor* needs, but I'm not much of a shopper. Besides, I like it. I think my animal heads will be right at home. You have excellent taste, Miss Willems."

"Stop calling me Miss Willems. My name is Stefani! I'm not your kindergarten teacher," she chastised, and his irrepressible, annoying grin appeared again.

"I don't want another house, Miss Willems. This one suits me just fine. I'm thinking the buffalo head will go right there." He held up his thumbs together and focused on a spot over the mantel. Stefani could only hope he was joking.

"I've lived in this area my entire life; I'll help you find another place." Her voice bordered on pleading, possibly pathetic. She had no room for pride. She wanted this house. At this point, she wasn't above groveling.

"I already have a real estate agent, and more importantly, I already have a house. Or at least I will in a few minutes," he checked his watch. "So I appreciate your offer, Miss Willems, but my answer is no," Mr. Savitch answered. "But I have to say I admire your persistence. You're a right pushy little thing." He smiled that infuriating grin again.

Stefani took in a quick breath to speak but could think of nothing to say. "Stefani, let's go. Your deposit is being refunded. I have a check at the office. We have no reason to bother Mr. Savitch further." George took her by the arm once again, but Stefani remained steadfast, looking to the stranger hopefully.

Stefani mustered up humility from deep within and took out a business card, handing it to the tall, handsome enemy. "If you change your mind, this is where I can be reached. My home phone is on the back, but I'm usually at work. I hope to hear from you," she smiled her sweetest smile and walked out the front door, clicking her heels on the beloved Mexican tile. George followed closely behind.

Stefani turned and stopped him in his tracks. "George, how could you? How could you let this house get away from me? You know what this land means to me!"

"Stefani, I have been trying to reach you since last night—and all morning. Your voice mail at work is full, you weren't home, you didn't answer any of my pages, and your secretary said you were out of the office until tomorrow. What was I supposed to do? I don't have the authority to make a more substantial offer without your approval or signature. You knew this deal was taking place today; if it was so important to you, why didn't you let someone know where you were?"

Stefani solemnly answered, "We had a power failure at the Sacramento site. All the computers were down and I had to fly there last night. I just got back this morning." Stefani let out a muffled cry. *Of all the days to have a disaster at work, why did it have to be now?*

"Well, Stefani, Mr. Savitch's offer came in this morning and I didn't have any authority to counter after his bid came across the wire. You know how Bay Area real estate is: You snooze, you lose."

"So that's it, I'm not the owner?" She tried to process the notion.

"I'm afraid not. Our offer was null and void because it expired before Mr. Savitch's came in." George shrugged. "Why don't we get an early dinner; we'll find something else soon." They both knew the statement was a lie. There was nothing else but this property. Nothing else that would prove to her parents she was successful. Nothing else that would keep her promise to her deceased grandmother. Her goal had slipped from her grasp into the hands of a handsome bachelor who didn't seem to care where he lived. The irony of it threatened to stifle her.

"Thanks for the dinner offer, but I couldn't eat a thing. I just want to get back to work and make this whole day just disappear." She definitely needed to pray about her situation. Her attitude toward Mr. Savitch was anything but Christian, and the truth was, Stefani was really angry with God.

George simply nodded in understanding. Obviously, he didn't want to pressure her for fear of losing a future sale. Stefani sulked to her car and hunkered down in the driver's seat, then sat looking at the house wistfully. *Why, God? I've finally given up the dream of marriage, a family, so why did You deny me this house? It's such a small thing in the scheme of this lifetime; I just don't understand. If I'm going to be an old maid, can't I at least be one in style?* She dropped her head to the steering wheel, but looked up at the unexpected sound of voices.

The bachelor's real estate agent had arrived. The pair walked the perimeter of the home. They talked of landscaping ideas and final finishing work. All details *she* should have been discussing with her agent.

Stefani wondered what Mr. Savitch did for a living. When he removed his hat, his hair was meticulously combed and his face clean-shaven, but he wore a tired chambray shirt around his broad chest with worn-out jeans on his long legs, with the beginnings of a hole in the knee apparent. The topper was the scuffed leather boots he wore. Stefani couldn't remember the last time that she'd seen a man wear boots in northern California. Or casual jeans for that matter—and never without a braided belt and matching loafers. It simply wasn't done in the engineering world of Silicon Valley.

"He looks ridiculous," she mumbled, lying aloud to herself. He looked striking, just like a spiffed-up, rugged, rodeo hero. A real rodeo hero, not the phony urban cowboy type. And she knew it; she just couldn't stand to admit it. It was bad enough he'd taken her house. Couldn't he at least have been ugly? Petty and small as it sounded, it would have made her feel better. She gave one last look at the house and then to the tall, gorgeous enemy. She sighed aloud.

It wouldn't take him long to find a renter. Once prospective tenants got a look at him, they'd probably be throwing money his way. He noticed her staring and threw her a friendly wave. She grimaced and started her car. She meandered back to the office. *Defeated.*

When she returned to her cubicle, her coworkers had prepared a party with balloons and a cake that read, "Congratulations on your New Home, Stefani!" She was utterly humiliated as she explained her loss and how it came about.

Her secretary and lifetime friend, Amy, smiled, obviously recognizing all was not right. Amy sweetly took Stefani aside and put an arm around her. "And we know that all things work together for good to them that love God."

Stefani forced a smile. There was nothing worse than having Scripture quoted casually when you felt at your lowest. Stefani knew Amy didn't mean harm by it, but it annoyed her just the same. She didn't want to hear how she *should* feel, when she was so down. God *knew* what the land had meant to her.

He must have made a mistake. It was just salt in the wound to be reminded that she should feel grateful. She didn't feel grateful, she felt angry and ignored by God. *Why would He let that man—that savage in the cowboy boots—buy her house?* It was a complete mystery to her, one that would probably never be answered in this lifetime. She couldn't fathom ever looking back on this day and being glad for its outcome.

two

John Savitch looked at the business card he held. *Stefani Willems, MIS Manager*. He had no idea what an MIS manager earned, but Stefani worked for a well-known company and she obviously had the money to buy the duplex, so she must have reached a modicum of success. He scanned the card again, debating. It had been three days. Three days and he couldn't erase her penetrating blue eyes from his memory. That pert nose or that exasperating, fake, doe-eyed smile when she thought she might change his mind.

Stefani's dark hair had been shaped into a short, serious cut. He imagined if she let it grow, she wouldn't appear so stern. But maybe MIS managers needed to be stern for all he knew. Even with her serious haircut, she was darling. The type of woman who would forever be described as cute, no matter how old she got. She looked about twenty-four, but he guessed she had to be older than that to afford the duplex. He admired her spunk. For some odd reason Stefani Willems wanted his house and badly. He couldn't help but want to know why.

She didn't think much of him. John knew better than to chase after some successful businesswoman with her mind set on material things. He was a simple farm boy at heart. Always would be, no matter how prosperous he became. Everything about Stefani's appearance screamed that work was her whole life: the conservative navy suit, the muted makeup, the haircut—and especially the dejection when she didn't get the duplex.

Just when he'd start to forget their meeting, he'd picture the sweet dimples, well worn into her naturally rosy cheeks. They belied her severe front and gave her true nature away. One thing was certain; he wanted to see more of *that* Stefani

Willems. Even though he knew better.

I'm making a sound business decision, he reminded himself. *She's the only person I know here and she can afford this*. Knowing full well that it was just a good excuse to call Stefani Willems, he inflated his chest with a deep breath and dialed the phone number on the card. To his surprise, she answered immediately, "This is Stefani."

"Miss Willems? It's John Savitch, the buyer for—"

"I know who you are, Mr. Savitch. What can I do for you? Have you decided against the duplex?" Hope resounded in her question.

"No, actually I have a proposition for you. Are you free for dinner tonight?"

She gave a long, annoyed sigh. "Mr. Savitch, your charms, while they may be irresistible to most women, are lost on me. If you need to start your harem here in California, perhaps you might start at the local singles' bar," she said sarcastically, but surprisingly she didn't hang up.

John stared at his receiver, unable to believe such a sweet little face with the innocent dimples could contain such a biting personality. He had thought her original reaction to him was just due to the shock of losing the house, but now he wondered. Had he been wrong about her? Maybe that spark he'd noticed between them was only in his overactive imagination.

He let out a short laugh. "Miss Willems, I have a legitimate business deal I'd like to discuss with you. While I'm sure you have men beating down your door for dates, that's not my sole intention. Are you available for dinner tonight? Trust me, you'll be safe," he added, possibly with more irritation than necessary. Everything that came out of her mouth was in sharp contrast to what he felt when he was with her—that feeling that they knew each other, understood one another.

"I can't leave the office until seven; I need to ensure that everything is online after a small issue we had here. Is a late dinner all right?" She sounded like she was doing *him* a favor.

John couldn't help his smile. "How's eight? I'll meet you at the restaurant of your choice." Her elegant navy suit wafted through his memory. No doubt she'd pick someplace that registered as a dining establishment.

"Eight o'clock. Stern's in Sunnyvale." Her voice had softened just the slightest bit. John hoped that tonight he'd get her to drop her cold front altogether.

"I'll be there," he promised and hung up the phone.

He dressed in a navy European suit with his yellow power tie. He checked his image in the hotel mirror before leaving. Satisfied, he stepped out of the elevator. The concierge stared strangely when John asked for directions to the restaurant. But the hotelier was used to seeing John in boots, so he was probably stunned by the dining choice. He hoped the meal would cost less than his suit.

After Miss Willems' reluctant acceptance, John arrived at the restaurant early so she'd have no excuses to miss their meeting. Doing Miss Stefani Willems a favor wouldn't be easy. Still, she had the ability to solve his problem and he had the ability to solve hers, so their meeting made sense.

From the parking lot, the restaurant didn't look too fancy. It was an old, almost dilapidated redwood-sided building. The sign above the doorway had fallen off one side, so it hung ominously. He figured the restaurant must have been a hangout for locals like Stefani. It probably had wonderful food, but lacked the elitist environment.

Although he was in the heart of the city, the parking lot was filled with pickups. It was a welcome sight, but something told him it wasn't a good sign. For a moment, John was reminded of an old *Twilight Zone* episode. He opened the spring-action door and it screeched painfully. Once inside, he burst into a hearty laugh. Loud bluegrass music emanated from every corner. The plank floor was covered wall-to-wall with sawdust, and neon signs illuminated the place. Over the music, a few patrons screamed their support for a would-be cowboy on the gyrating mechanical bull.

Couples whirled upon the dance floor. Full jean skirts and

ruffled cotton tops flittered under the neon lights. Western attire ruled. John felt the judgmental stares and realized he looked ridiculous in his business suit and dress shoes. Stefani Willems certainly had a way of getting her point across.

Stefani entered the establishment and bit her lip, apparently to hold back her laughter. Scanning John, she obviously enjoyed her little joke. Her blue eyes sparkled with merriment. Despite her desperate attempts, her charming dimples kept appearing and she finally let out her giggle at his expense. "I'm sorry," she covered her mouth with her slender, graceful hands to stifle her laughter. "I'm sorry."

"Go ahead, get it all out," he said stiffly.

"I just wanted you to feel comfortable," she explained, batting her eyelashes in mock innocence.

He wagged his finger at her. "Uh-huh, I'm sure my comfort level was the first thing on your mind. One day, the right man will ask you to wear jeans and a pair of boots and you're going to love it! Until then, we're out of here." He took her by the hand and led her to his car. Stefani's figure was made for jeans, he thought, as he eyed her small frame in a summer-white business suit. Her skirt was a couple of inches above her knees. Heaven help him, she had beautiful legs.

"Where are we going?" she demanded. She wriggled her hand free.

"We're going somewhere my suit will be appreciated. It isn't every day I dress up for a woman. And it isn't going to waste."

"I'm not riding in that!" she protested, as though the truck was beneath her. John had a feeling she'd never admit to liking anything about him. Something about that fact challenged him. Delighted him.

"You should have thought of that before you thought up this little scheme of yours, Miss Willems. If you wanted me to know you think I'm a hick, consider your message delivered. Now, do you want to hear my offer or not? Not that you deserve it."

"Yes, I want to hear it." She rolled her eyes.

"Then get in." He opened the door for her and she climbed up, carefully ensuring she kept her legs as covered as possible. John shut the door behind her and got into the leather driver's seat. Country music blasted from the stereo when he started the car. From the corner of his eye, he saw she was rolling those big blue eyes again.

He turned off the stereo and hummed the theme song "Green Acres" just to annoy her.

"Where are we going?" she asked curtly, interrupting his song.

"I don't know. Where can you get a good side of ribs around here, the kind with lots of sauce?" He studied her white suit and she smiled, despite herself. "Glad to see you can still smile, Miss Willems. Do you always get up on the wrong side of the bed?"

"I don't like it when things don't go the way I planned," she explained.

"I can see that."

"You want me to apologize, don't you?" Her blue eyes thinned.

He shrugged. "Nope. Not unless you want to. Far be it from me to make a spoiled child behave properly when she isn't mine."

"Spoiled child? I'll have you know I haven't been spoiled a day in my life."

"Maybe that's because you don't allow people to spoil you," he responded evenly.

She crossed her arms. "I don't want to be spoiled."

"Everyone wants to be spoiled once in a while."

She looked up at him and he thought he saw a tear, but she blinked it away quickly and turned toward the window. Silence hung between them until they arrived at a small French restaurant. John had interviewed for his California job there. It was slightly romantic for either occasion, but he didn't know of anything else, so that left few options.

He drove into the parking lot of the quaint little bistro. He looked around at all the foreign luxury cars and figured his suit was safe here. He watched the surprise in her eyes when she noted the restaurant. She obviously was familiar with it.

"This place is expensive," she said flatly. She might have been concerned for him, but her tone told him she didn't want to be embarrassed if his credit card was rejected.

"Us country bumpkins can afford to splurge once in a while." The corners of his mouth curved. "We can even spoil our friends when the occasion allows." He helped her from the car and they walked the short distance to the entrance.

"That duplex isn't cheap; you'd have a lot more financial freedom if you decided not to buy. I could purchase half the duplex; you could buy dinner. What do you think?"

"You are relentless." He turned his attention to the maitre d' as they entered the quiet, candlelit restaurant. "Two for dinner, please."

"Yes, sir." The Frenchmen led them to a cozy table in the corner.

John was pleased with the romantic ambiance. *It's been too long since I've had a date.* Too bad Stefani had no reason to call it a date. She perused him, studied his suit, and then looked at his face once again.

She appeared accustomed to such restaurants, and why not? Clearly she was an elegant woman, well dressed and educated. Still, something about her told him she had worked hard for that image. While John could hold his own in the manners department, he would have preferred the slab of ribs he'd referred to earlier.

She covered her lap with the linen napkin and spoke. "So, this proposition you have for me?" she asked pointedly, her blue eyes blazing.

"Can we order first? I prefer discussing business on a full stomach. I'm not such bad company, you know?"

"I'm sure you're not, but I'm without a place to live soon, so I'm afraid that's my priority. To be more direct, your house is my priority."

John was rankled; he held up his hands, signaling defeat. "It's a building—four walls. How could you possibly be so attached to an object? Did you ever stop to think I might be an exceptionally nice guy and you're missing out on a great evening?" He tossed the linen napkin on the table in disgust.

"You seem pretty attached to the duplex yourself, Mr. Savitch. Enough to outbid me and buy it out from under my nose." She sat back in her chair, crossing her arms. Other patrons were starting to stare. They looked like an old, antagonistic couple rather than two people on a first date. But of course, it wasn't a date. Stefani had made that perfectly clear.

"I made an offer fair and square. It's not my fault you don't keep in touch with your real estate agent." *What am I doing? I'm starting to sound just like her!* He sucked in a deep breath and said a quick prayer for his even temper to return. "Look, Miss Willems, I didn't come here to argue with you. Let's enjoy a nice dinner together. Surely, you can put up with me for one meal. I won't bother ordering a soufflé for dessert." He let the corner of his mouth turn and he noticed her dimples had appeared in full for the first time since their acquaintance.

Her dimples were gorgeous, the perfect accompaniment to her sweet, rosy cheeks and sparkling, wide eyes. Why on earth she chose to keep them under wraps for so long was beyond him. No matter what she thought of him, he felt her attraction. It was unstated, but undeniable. A force of chemistry unexplainable and bonding.

She looked up from her down-turned chin and her long, black lashes batted coquettishly. Not consciously, though. Clearly she thought she appeared threatening, but her innocent features made her harsh nature almost comical.

"You're right, I'm sorry," she answered weakly. "We'll have a nice dinner." He noticed her eyes remained on his own and she scrutinized him, not in her standard, calculated way, but in a soft, thoughtful way. *What does she think of me? And why on earth does she care so much about a house?*

The waiter brought water and menus. Stefani grabbed the folder quickly; she clearly relished something to hide behind. She opened her menu wide and her features disappeared. When she didn't emerge for some time, he cleared his throat. "Do you speak French, Miss Willems?"

She dropped the menu to the table in defeat, letting out a long, deep sigh. "No."

"Would you like some suggestions?" he asked gently.

"I'm sure the waiter can help me," Stefani squared her shoulders, but then grimaced nervously, her self-confidence clearly waning. "I like chicken," she said meekly. "Do they have chicken on this menu?"

He put his hand to hers and noticed she jumped. "I know the perfect dish."

The waiter returned, putting on his best airs to make patrons feel intimidated. John wished he knew of another restaurant, but since he didn't, he used his best French to order their meals. The waiter glared at John as though the American accent was more than the server could bear. John folded the menus and handed them back, concentrating on Stefani.

"Thank you," she said, her voice barely above a whisper.

"The restaurant may be expensive, but the attitude is included at no extra charge." He laughed out loud and she joined him. The waiter gave them a cold stare, which only made them laugh again.

"I'm sorry I took you to the sawdust palace. I didn't mean to be uncivilized, I was just angry. Childish. . . Anyway, I'm sorry. I'm mad at my situation and I took it out on you."

"The fact is that place is right up my alley. Ain't nothing wrong with a good night of cowboy music, and don't you roll those pretty blue eyes at me, princess. You give it a shot before you knock it." He cleared his throat. "So what is an MIS manager?" John asked innocently.

"An MIS manager is someone that reports to the vice president with data on all information systems infrastructure and its components."

"That's kind of vague. You want to help me out here?"

"I coordinate the equipment needs for all the departments. I help them decide which computer systems will work best and eliminate the ones that don't work well."

"Ahhh."

"And what is it you do, Mr. Savitch? You own a suit; I suppose that's a good sign." She leaned in, setting her elbow on the table.

"Do you always say whatever you're thinking?" He met her blue eyes with his own and challenged her. She looked away quickly. He loved that she said what she thought. It was refreshing. Stefani Willems had more in common with him than she thought. Neither of them pulled any punches.

"As a matter of fact, I do say what I'm thinking," she said with an apologetic tone. "No sense in playing games. It's dishonest and annoying as far as I'm concerned." She shrugged. "It's just the way I am. I don't want to offend you, but that house is very special to me and—and I want to live there."

He saw her eyes glisten with moisture. The sight of true sentiment brought out his most tender feelings. Glory, she was beautiful—and too busy with her agenda to ever notice. If she had noticed, she wouldn't have chopped away all her hair. He wanted to tell her, whisper in her delicate ear that there was more to life than houses. More to life than business, but he swallowed hard and sat up straight.

"Stefani," he whispered. Her eyes snapped to his once again with the intimacy of her first name. *She had noticed.* "Stefani, I want you to rent the other half of the duplex. I know it's not the same as owning it, but if that's what you truly want, to *live* there, I'm giving you the opportunity. And if I decide to sell, you'll get the first option to buy."

Her head nodded up and down in slow motion. "Yes." It came out as a mere breath and John wished he might kiss her soft, full lips at the delicious word. Something was definitely happening between them. He could tell she didn't want to acknowledge it, but it was there just the same.

three

Boxes were strewn about the new house. Stacked, full, and everywhere. A constant reminder of all she had to do. *I thought I worked all the time, but apparently I had a little time for shopping*. Friends from church had moved her things to the new house in various pickups and vans. After a quick lunch of pizza and soda, everyone had slowly gone home and Stefani was left alone to unpack.

The flower-box kitchen window held a perfect view of John's half of the house. She slowly made her way to the window. The professional movers had finished at John's house, too, and his open garage was filled to capacity. Stefani sighed at the seemingly endless amount of work and began taking out her dishes, one by one, rinsing them in the sink.

John emerged from his garage with a newspaper, a chaise lounge, and a tall glass filled with iced tea. He wore sunglasses, a T-shirt that framed his muscular chest, and a pair of athletic shorts. His long, powerful legs caught Stefani's attention and she felt herself gulp when he turned and caught her gawking at him. He waved casually and motioned for her to come outside. He pulled out his chaise in their shared driveway and made himself comfortable. "He's just going to sit there," she stated to herself.

For the life of her, she didn't know why, but she wiped her hands on a towel and went outside. Perhaps it was her own guilt for treating him so badly. She stood over him, sheltering her eyes from the sun. "Don't you have to unpack? You're just going to sit here?" she asked incredulously.

"Why not? This is my favorite time of day. Right before the sun goes down and the cool, evening breeze from the Bay comes inland. It's too good to miss. We don't have this moist air back home." He took a deep, audible breath. "Smell that air. It's something to be experienced. Join me; I'll get another tea and a lounger." He started to get up and she pushed his shoulder back down.

"Don't bother. I can't lounge; I've got an entire house to put away! And so do you."

He shrugged. "This sunset will only happen once. God will never make one exactly like it again." He lifted his tea glass toward the reddish-orange sun on the horizon behind the mountains.

She wondered if he was a believer or just making light of God's creation. His lackadaisical attitude appalled her, but Lord help her, she desired to relax like that. To sit and sip tea with him until the sun came up again. If only she knew how to relax. John Savitch captivated her, even though she knew his type was off-limits. His laziness would only serve in her favor. She'd get the house back quicker. "I–I can't, thanks. My friends all went home and I've got a million things to do."

"It'll all be there tomorrow," he encouraged. "Sit with me."

"I've got church tomorrow."

"Ah, so you're a churchgoing woman." He took a long drink from his glass. Mortified by her earlier behavior, especially taking him to the sawdust-ridden country café, she was now embarrassed to admit her faith—and she should be. She hadn't acted like a churchgoing woman.

"I am a Christian, although there are times I don't act like it. What about you?" she asked tentatively, swallowing hard. If he wasn't a Christian, she'd done nothing to further her faith with him.

"Born again in 1978," he stated with conviction.

"Seventy-eight? How old are you? I'm sorry, that was rude. I'm not always obnoxious." *Just whenever I open my mouth.*

"The word obnoxious never crossed my mind. I like a woman who says what she thinks. For the record, I'm thirty-five. Does that make me too old? Too young? What?" he asked. She had a feeling his question was a leading one.

"Are you asking how old I am?"

"Heavens, no. A gentleman would never ask that."

"Good, but I'm thirty-two." She felt herself smile. Upon learning he was a Christian, Stefani suddenly felt worse for the treatment. It didn't show her Christianity in the most positive light.

John stood and motioned for her to sit in his chaise lounge. She pointed back at her house. All the things she had to do. . . Against her better judgment, she sat down, anyway. He grabbed another chair from the garage and sat beside her. His head was slightly behind her and she had a full view of his long, muscular legs once again—this time in close proximity. *Whatever he does to keep in shape, it sure works.*

She wasn't the type to gawk at men, but John Savitch wasn't just any man physically. Cowboys weren't her type; she liked men in business suits. But the fact remained: This guy would look good in full waders.

She stopped herself, remembering not only was this her landlord, but the man who held her dream house within his reach. Christian or not, he didn't seem like the marrying type. Stefani's mother had warned her about handsome men and it was the one piece of advice Stefani had taken to heart. It didn't mean anything that she found him good-looking. It was just a fact.

John Savitch was nothing more than an attractive obstacle. And she'd find a way to remove it. A tiny sports car sputtered into the driveway. Stefani looked at John apologetically. "I'm sorry, that's my secretary. I guess she came back to help." Stefani rose from the chaise lounge. "Thanks for the chair. I hope you enjoy the sunset."

"Your secretary must be committed to her boss," he replied. "Coming over on a Saturday and all."

"Oh, no, we're friends first. We've known each other since school. She's only been my secretary for a year. I shouldn't have called her that. I'd better get back to work. Nice chatting with you. It looks like you could get busy yourself." She nodded toward the garage.

"When the sun disappears, I will." Even his voice was relaxed.

She rolled her eyes. That's why she liked businessmen; they were committed to getting things done. This guy had probably never even set a goal, much less achieved one.

"Amy, hi," Stefani called.

Amy ignored Stefani completely and held her hand out to John. "Hi, I'm Amy."

"Pleasure to meet you. I'm John Savitch. Tell Stefani to take a break and enjoy the sunset with me. I'll get you both some tea."

Amy turned, her blond hair flailing wildly. "We should enjoy the sunset, Stefani," she urged her friend through clenched teeth.

Stefani simply smiled and grabbed Amy by the hand, dragging her into the new house. "Come on, we've got work to do. Enjoy the view, John."

"I will," he said, as he watched her walk away.

Once inside the house, Amy went straight to the kitchen window. "How can you possibly think about working when you've got *him*," she sighed the last word, "in your driveway?"

"Amy, get away from the window. We're not in high school anymore."

"Are you kidding? I'd pay rent just for that view, forget this house. What does he do for a living? Must be something physical, judging by that body."

"Amy! Mind your manners. You're a Christian woman! You sound like you're at a singles' bar."

"Sorry, you're right, but I don't think I have ever seen one quite like him before. Is he a contractor? He built this house, right?"

"I have no idea what he does for a living and I don't think he's going to tell me either. He thinks I'm a snob. I'm sure whatever it is, he doesn't use his mind."

"You? A snob? Goodness, I wonder what ever gave him that idea. Stefani, you didn't show him your business attitude? Tell me you didn't." Stefani shifted uneasily on her feet, a guilty expression crossing her face. "Stefani! Look at him!" Amy pulled her over to the window and yanked her chin so Stefani was facing John Savitch's profile.

Oh, my, but he does look good. "Looks aren't everything, Amy. Besides, he's not my type. He usually dresses like a cowboy. Boots. . .the whole thing. I like businessmen, suits. . . a man that knows how to treat a woman. If Mama taught me one thing, it's that a man who looks *that* good can only mean trouble. Give me an accountant any day."

"Stefani, just because someone wears a suit, it doesn't make him a gentleman. Most women like men that look rugged, men that have a little muscle on them."

"Most women probably think John Savitch is the ultimate male, so they can have him. Personally, I don't want any man, but I especially don't want a cowboy. I want this house and one day, when John decides to settle down with one of his little fillies, this house will be mine. Like it should have been in the first place." Stefani pulled away from Amy's grip to avoid looking at John's physique for a moment longer.

"So where does one sign up to be one of the fillies?" Amy winked, but her smile left when Stefani threw her a chastising glare. "All right, I'm just kidding. Besides, I'm sure he's not a Christian anyway."

"Actually, he is," Stefani relayed. "Said he was born-again."

"If he's too good to be true, sign me up as an investigative reporter to find out the truth."

"Amy! Did you come to help or not?" Stefani threw her fists to her hips in mock anger. "You act as though you've never seen a man before. Just like when we were in high school."

"Oh, chill out, I'm just kidding. You saw him first, so you have dibs. Even if you don't realize you want them yet. Come on, let's start upstairs and get your bedroom ready. I imagine those legs look pretty good from up there." They both broke into a giggle and climbed the stairs with boxes in hand. "What do you have in here?" Amy complained.

The two women laughed like schoolgirls as they put Stefani's clothes away. The sun dropped and Amy sighed with disappointment to find John long gone from the driveway when she was ready to leave. "Ah, well, I suppose I'll be seeing more of him if he's going to be your landlord."

"Don't call him that. Someday, I will own this house and John Savitch will be nothing but a memory to it."

"Right, Stef, I'm sure he's just going to move out of his *house* because you want it. It must be nice, living in that little fantasy world you've made for yourself." Amy laughed at her own joke. "See you tomorrow at church. Do you want me to pick you up?"

"Nah, I'll want to get back home quickly so I can finish unpacking. I'll see you there. Thanks for all your help."

"No problem." Amy pulled out from the driveway and called from her open window. "And be nice to your landlord or it may be *you* that's the memory around here. Staple that mouth shut if you have to."

Stefani tossed her hand at Amy. As Stefani turned to go back in the house, she noticed orange and red flames bursting within John's darkened kitchen. Frantic and acting on pure adrenaline, she ran to her garage and grabbed the fire extinguisher that came with the house. She broke the kitchen window with the back end of the extinguisher and pointed the black hose at a burner on the stove, which was submerged in a small, yet full flame. A loud fizzle sounded. Within a matter of seconds the blaze was gone and replaced with a white, sudsy mess. Stefani rushed into the unlocked back door to ensure she'd gotten the entire fire. John stood beside her clapping slowly. "Bravo."

Stefani was indignant. "What are you doing? That's a gourmet stove! Do you have any idea how much that thing cost? Certainly, you're bright enough to take care of this house!" Stefani shook her head, exasperated that anyone could be so careless.

"Stefani, I know you're prone to saying what you think, but *that* was uncalled for." His voice held none of his usual masculine charm.

"You're setting my stove on fire and you're going to tell me I'm rude?"

"It's *my* stove, Stefani."

"I picked it out," she shot back. Reality slapped her. It was *his* stove and *his* house and *his* idiot mistake. And it wasn't hers to worry about, *yet*. She tried to recover a shred of dignity. "Regardless of whose stove it is, I don't think setting fire to it is a good idea either way. Give it a few days maybe." She held her chin high. "You haven't even had time to let the insurance take effect," she mumbled under her breath, casting a sideways glance at the broken window and fire extinguisher residue.

"I tried to light the pilot light and, apparently, the gas was running too long. I would have handled it, Stefani. I was a volunteer firefighter before I finished college."

"You went to college?" She hadn't meant to sound indignant, but that's exactly how it came out.

"Yeah, believe it or not, we have a few of them in Colorado. Us hicks gotta get educated." His sarcastic tone told her he was still angry. "We even have a city or two out there, believe it or not. But, I kin understand you city folks wouldn't know nuthin' about that," he replied in a fake drawl.

Stefani turned on her heels. She faced him with all her venom. "It wouldn't kill you to say 'thank you.' "

"Thank you?" he shouted. "For what? Breaking my window? Dousing my stove? Or for coming into my house and calling me stupid?" He held his hands open toward her, like she owed him an apology.

"I didn't call you stupid." Stefani was shocked at his accusation. She'd said nothing of the kind. She'd thought it, but she'd said nothing of the kind. She actually had congratulated herself for showing restraint.

"You might as well have called me stupid. What is it that frustrates you so much about me, Stefani?"

That you're gorgeous, you own my house, you're a cowboy, and I still find you incredibly attractive. "Nothing. You could have set the houses on fire!" she added. "In case you have forgotten, I live next door."

"I didn't set the houses on fire," he reminded her.

"Thanks to me." She held up the extinguisher.

"I'm glad to know I have an expert in fire prevention living next door. Why are you so angry at the world, Stefani?"

"I'm not angry at the world." *Just you.*

He motioned to the coffeemaker on the opposite counter. "Do you want a cup of coffee?" His tone wasn't necessarily inviting, but it was the least she could do after she'd put her foot in her mouth, yet again. When would she ever learn to control her outbursts? Getting on John's bad side would serve no purpose at all.

"Coffee sounds great." She remembered the verse she knew so well about even the fool being thought wise when quiet. If only she could live it. Offending him would get her nowhere. Why did she have such a difficult time remembering such a simple task?

Stefani walked into the living room and stopped in her tracks at the sight of the furniture. Inside the elegantly traditional Mediterranean home he'd placed a sofa that defied explanation. At one time it was obviously a bright turquoise floral print, but from its many years of use, it had become a pallid blue. Only a few specks of turquoise remained: elements of past grandeur, reminders of days long gone.

He'd placed the atrocity in the center of the room, even though it had no back on it whatsoever. Just a big hole that showed its sofa guts. Just like a sample on a showroom floor. He might have at least put it up against the wall or thrown something over it. Stefani searched for a pleasant comment, but nothing came. She snapped her gaping mouth shut.

John brought out a cup of coffee and with it the dreaded

words she feared: "Have a seat."

As much as she wanted to keep quiet, her mouth resisted. "Why on earth would you move that thing across two states?"

"You know how long that sofa's been with me?"

"Please don't tell me you were *born* on it." Stefani cracked.

"Sit down. I had it cleaned just before I moved. I promise. And I've only had it since college."

She sat down with her coffee. "Well, it's comfortable and when you're sitting in it, you don't have to look at it." She fidgeted into the back of the couch and he sat down beside her.

"*I've* only had it since college, but it was a hand-me-down from a friend that got it at a secondhand store."

"Why do I not find that the least bit surprising?"

"This couch is ten feet long. It's hard to find a sofa this long anymore and when you're as tall as I am, that's important."

"You just bought a duplex worth a small fortune, but you can't afford a new couch?"

"I just bought a duplex worth a small fortune," he repeated, "so no I can't. Well, I probably could if I raised the rent next door." He smiled and hid behind his coffee cup.

"Very funny. If this place is such a stretch for you, you might consider something more affordable," she suggested, but he saw right through her ruse. His friendly manner turned. His smiling eyes disappeared.

"Stefani, you can think of me as your enemy forever, but it won't change your situation. God didn't give you this house for a reason, so stop blaming me. I don't know what His reason is, but I imagine someday you will. Until that day, be thankful for what you have."

He put his mug down with a bang on the coffee table. She'd made him angry again. With her characteristic, say-anything style, she was used to offending people. But with John it bothered her. Perhaps because he was so difficult to offend. Stefani actually went out of her way to do it. It didn't speak well of her and she didn't like that feeling one bit. She felt like her mother.

"I am thankful for what I have, but I still want this house. I'm sorry, but I just can't see any reason God would deny me this house. Do you know how long I worked for this? Only to have it stolen from me at the last possible minute? Do you have any idea how frustrating that is?"

His eyes softened. "I'm sure it is, but maybe God wants to give you something else, something better. And the house is not gone; you're living in it. The fact that you can afford to live in one of the best areas in one of America's most expensive real estate markets shows just how spoiled you are." John took the coffee cup from her and went to the kitchen. Apparently, their conversation was over. Stefani stood abruptly.

"You think I'm spoiled?" she called after him, squaring her shoulders. "Well, cowboy, I've worked hard for everything I have. Why shouldn't I have this house? No one gave me a thing!"

He walked purposely from the kitchen and wrapped her up in an unexpected embrace. Stefani felt like a rag doll in his arms and she didn't know how to react. He nudged her chin upward with his thumb, forcing her to look into the depths of his eyes. She heard herself whimper.

His eyes flickered. "God never promised us happiness. He promised to take care of us. . .to meet our *needs.* And I'd say your needs are more than met. The happiness factor is up to you," he whispered forcefully, as he held her in his arms firmly.

She was face-to-face with those green eyes. Any hope of normalcy was lost. All her anger, her frustration seemed to disappear and transform into hope. The armored exterior she wore was stripped away in his warmth—by the deep, inexplicable awareness they had for one another.

He spoke again, still whispering. "You've got a lot of friends; I saw them helping you today, so I know you're capable of holding that tongue of yours. Could you at least try to be civil to me? To get your mind off your housing agenda for one minute?"

Even close up, she failed to find a flaw on him. She nodded

slowly, unable to let out her breath. She closed her eyes, unwilling to stare into those green eyes a moment longer. *I don't like cowboys. I don't like cowboys*, she reminded herself. His grip tightened on her arms and he pulled her into a kiss. She melted into it, becoming painfully aware that she'd never been kissed like this before. His kiss was unfaltering, confident, and it made her knees buckle.

He held her jaw gently and she went forward toward his kiss. Perhaps she'd been wrong about cowboys. She'd certainly been wrong about John. He pulled away and her lips remained puckered, desperately wanting another kiss, but he straightened his back and dropped his arms.

"That's better," he commented before he started emptying a nearby moving box.

"Better than what?" she asked in confusion.

"Better than your mouth constantly berating me. I'm glad to know it has other attributes." He smiled assuredly. If she weren't so numbed she would have slapped him. He continued to put things away, completely ignoring her presence. *After he just kissed me. . .like that!* Stefani stood motionless. Obviously, the kiss had meant nothing to him; it was just a way to shut her up.

Apparently, kissing women casually came easy to him. The idea sickened her. John Savitch had her house and now he had something else: a portion of her heart. She wished she could take that kiss back to show him he meant nothing to her. Unfortunately, her body still clamored for another kiss—denying how she *should* feel.

She huffed a desperate, short sigh and ran to her house, utterly humiliated. He'd proved his point: She was weak and he'd won the house for a reason. Well, she wouldn't let him get the better of her again. She was stronger willed than he was, and she'd prove it. She'd spent a lifetime studying the reasons to keep away from a man like him. Now it was time to put what she'd learned to good use.

four

Stefani wrestled all night with her pillow; she socked it a few times in frustration. How had she let it happen? A kiss, to a man she barely knew. A man who stood in her way. She had always been in complete control of her emotions. How on earth could a cowboy manage to tear away the guard she'd carefully managed her entire life? It had just been a long time since she'd kissed a man, she reasoned. But it only made John's fiery kiss more vivid. She had *never* been kissed like that before.

With melancholy, she figured John probably had a lot of practice. She stared at her reflection in the mirror. *Would any man ever make me feel like that again?*

"Life isn't about feelings," she reminded herself. "Look how far your mother got on feelings."

Stefani resolved to get off to church early to avoid seeing John. If she couldn't avoid her own emotions, she could at least avoid him. The longer she didn't have to set eyes on John Savitch, the better. She dressed in her finest suit: a raspberry-toned ensemble with a conservative hemline and collared neckline. She stepped in front of the full-length mirror and sneered. *Has my haircut always been this way?* It was decidedly masculine. Boyish. Why hadn't she noticed before? Her bright blue eyes were lost in the haircut's severity.

"Blech!" she said to the mirror. *Vanity!* She threw down her brush in disgust, grabbed her Bible, and headed toward the garage.

She opened the garage door and nearly jumped out of her skin. John stood in the driveway, waiting with arms crossed, embracing a worn Bible. He wore a dark brown brushed leather jacket, jeans without kneeholes, and his clearly polished boots. She guessed he was trying to dress up.

He called out to her: "You own a pair of jeans, princess?"

"Yes?" she asked cautiously. "But I'm on my way to church; it *is* Sunday. Why do you ask?"

"Go grab your jeans. I want to show you something after church," he ordered.

"After church?"

"I'm tagging along. Since you didn't invite me, I'm inviting myself. I don't have a home church yet, so I'm sure you wouldn't mind if I tried yours." He shoved his hands into his leather jacket, tucked his Bible under his arm, and nodded at the brown duffel bag hanging on his shoulder.

"Actually, you're not really dressed for my church. It might be better if—"

"I'll be fine. Go get a pair of jeans and a sweater. Oh, and some shoes you can walk in, preferably boots." He motioned toward her heels and got into her car. He settled into her passenger seat.

Stefani leaned over the opened car window. "John, I don't *own* boots and there are hundreds of churches in the area. Wouldn't you be more comfortable at another one? I mean, we already live right next to one another."

"Don't they teach the Bible at your church?"

"Well, yes."

"Then that's as good a place as any to start. Did you want to take my car?" he asked, pointing back toward his own garage.

She sighed heavily. "No." She couldn't deny taking him to church. That bordered on unchristian. "But after church, I'm bringing you right home. I have a million things to do today. And throwing on a pair of jeans for anything, other than unpacking, is not on my agenda."

"I have something I want to show you. It's very special to me. Come on, it's Sunday. You're not supposed to be working today, anyway." He had her there.

Stefani suddenly reasoned whatever was so special to him might hold the key to his moving. Without further argument, she ran upstairs and grabbed a pair of jeans and a baby blue sweater. *He hasn't lived on the peninsula very long; perhaps he bought in a rush. Maybe there is a special place. . .* She could just casually look up listed homes and later mention an available house on the market. Her mind rambled with the possibilities. She picked up her running shoes in the garage and settled herself behind the steering wheel.

She glared at him. "You're accustomed to getting what you want, aren't you?" She broke into a knowing smile. *But so am I.*

"Hey, the Christian thing to do would have been to invite me to church. Especially after you kissed me like that last night." He riffled through her CDs and selected one, taking it out of its case.

Her smile disappeared. "Kissed you! John Savitch, you are incorrigible!"

He shrugged. "It's okay, I forgive you. I have that effect on women." He broke into a wide grin to show he was teasing, and despite herself, she wanted to kiss him again. *And on a Sunday!*

John's suave disposition managed to give the distinct impression she was the only woman in the world. Deep down, she knew men like him fell for gorgeous, flirtatious women. The kind that knew the right things to say at the right time. . . Attractive cowboys didn't fall for serious business types with trouble maintaining proper decorum in social situations. John was not falling for her. He was simply toying with her emotions.

"I'm taking you to church this morning because it's my Christian duty to help get you started church shopping, but after this, you're on your own." She tried to sound firm, knowing that if she didn't put a stop to his incessant flirting, he'd only break her heart. Strong willed or not, she wasn't made of stone.

"Well, thanks for performing your Christian duty."

"Speaking of which, don't you have a suit you could wear? My church is pretty formal." She leaned against the steering wheel, offering him one last chance to change.

"I've got my best boots on, what more do you want? This is what everyone wears to church where I come from. At least I shined my boots." He lifted up a foot then sat back into her passenger seat, showing he had no intention of changing his clothes. "Besides, how do I know you won't screech out of here and leave me?"

He had a point.

When they arrived at church, Stefani had never felt so popular. Every unattached woman she knew, whether casually or intimately, suddenly became a lot friendlier. Their interest in her landlord was more than obvious. She had to admit it: Her church wasn't exactly teeming with available Christian men. John seemed oblivious to the attention, and for that Stefani was thankful.

That is, until they were stopped in the foyer by a familiar face and a low, throaty voice. "Stefani, hi. I heard you moved. Who's this?" Rachel Cummings was one of the most beautiful women at the church and she knew it. She had red hair, green eyes, and a figure that seemed to come naturally. Stefani had to work out constantly to maintain a slim frame.

Rachel was one of those women whose eyes sparkled with intention and she always knew the right thing to say. The kind who had very few female friends because she dripped of something unspoken and brazen—the kind whose faith was always questioned by other women.

Rachel snuggled up to John easily, like a cat would to a cat-hater, completely ignoring Stefani's presence. Stefani felt her own claws come out and she realized she was actually feeling possessive of her handsome landlord. Stefani cleared her throat and made the introductions without ceremony or inflection. "Rachel, this is John Savitch, my landlord. John Savitch, Rachel Cummings."

"John," Rachel purred. "So nice to meet you. Stefani has told me all about you. Haven't you, Stefani?" she asked with raised eyebrows. Rachel tossed her red hair and Stefani felt the swinging strand cross her cheek with a quick sting. Rachel held her head cocked, looking up with her big green eyes and luscious, long eyelashes. Stefani inwardly wondered how many coats of mascara it took.

"Rachel, it's such a pleasure to meet you," John said in an exaggerated drawl. "Stefani hadn't mentioned you, but it's so nice to meet you. Any friend of Stefani's is a friend of mine, right, hon?" He slapped her back lightly and she coughed.

"Anything you say, pard'ner. When you get a job, maybe you and Rachel could get together sometime." Stefani grinned.

"There's no hurry. My welfare checks don't run out for a few months now, darling," John answered slyly.

Rachel gave a half smile while John took Stefani's arm and led her away from the church's beauty queen.

"Are you through?" Stefani asked him. "Welfare? Really, John."

"You jealous?" He smiled.

"Not in the least bit. As a matter of fact, I was just thinking you two deserved each other. Want her phone number?" Stefani asked sarcastically.

"Oh, you wound me so. No thanks; I don't like redheads. I'm partial to brunettes. Brunettes with darling dimples and an agenda they can't seem to forget about." John lowered his hand into her own and gave it a quick squeeze. "Call me a glutton for punishment."

She grimaced as they sat down in the pew and began to sing the first hymns of the morning. Stefani fidgeted throughout the sermon, which went completely over her head. She couldn't help but notice the attention they were attracting together. After the service ended, John pulled Stefani into the foyer before they had time to speak to anyone.

"Don't you want to meet the pastor?" Stefani asked.

"I can meet him anytime. Come on, I have a surprise for you. Go change into your jeans."

She did as she was told and emerged to find John waiting in his standard, rugged jeans and scuffed-up boots. "That's better." He clicked his tongue. "You were made for jeans, princess. I hope to see you in them more often." Again, he took her by the arm with all the chivalry of an English gentleman.

"Yep, we'll have to get you some boots."

"I like heels," she replied curtly.

Once in her car, he led her up into the hills and down several winding tree-lined roads before they came to a long asphalt driveway. Stefani had lived on the peninsula her entire life and had never seen the road taken. The car wound around the trees and she had to admit the park-like setting was incredibly serene.

"Park the car over there." He pointed to a white fence where several horses grazed in the distance.

She parked her car amidst the dust and coughed dramatically as she emerged from the car, waving her hand in front of her. "Now will you tell me why we're here?" Stefani had never heard such quiet. Even in their suburban neighborhood this kind of peace was unheard of. Everything was perfectly still. A distant whinny from a horse only soothed her frayed nerves. She took a deep breath and inhaled the rich eucalyptus scent that surrounded her. As much as she hated to admit it, it was beautiful. One thing was certain: John Savitch knew how to relax.

"I wanted you to meet Kayla," John answered and Stefani's peace was suddenly shattered.

Stefani looked at him like he'd just stepped out of a UFO. "You brought me out here to meet your girlfriend?"

"Not my girlfriend, my horse; Kayla's Pride and Joy. Kayla for short."

"Who's Kayla named after?" Stefani inquired uneasily.

"The gal who named the horse, I suppose." He shrugged.

"You didn't name your own horse?"

"The horse is named by the breeders. She's registered."

"For what, china? Is she getting married?"

"She's registered with the American Quarter Horse Association. Hang on a minute." He briefly disappeared into a stable and came out leading a magnificent horse by a ring and tether. "*This* is Kayla," he said proudly, beaming like a brand-new papa.

Stefani stepped back and gulped, "S–she's big."

"And the reason I don't own a better couch," he joked.

"This beauty costs me a bundle. You want a ride?"

Stefani's eyes grew wide. "No way. She looks like a racehorse. I've never even been on a pony, and quite frankly, I don't plan to get on one anytime soon." Stefani started to walk closer to her car. She was scared to death of large animals. A fact she chose to keep to herself.

He laughed at her. "Not a ride on Kayla, she's still young. Just three years old. She's still being trained. I'll get one of the gentle stable mares for you and we can ride together. Come on, it will be fun. Kayla needs the exercise."

"John, I still have an entire house to unpack." She looked back at him.

"Sunday is a day of rest. You would waste this gorgeous day unpacking?" He held up his hand to the blue sky.

"Resting and horseback riding are completely different things for me," she explained as she opened her car door. He pulled the horse and came toward her, sidling the oversized animal beside her, and she shivered.

"Look at those big brown eyes. You could refuse a face like this?" He patted Kayla on the short, wide nose and used his hip to shut the car door.

Stefani looked at the huge eyes on the mare. The horse was beautiful, truly noble in stature. Stefani didn't know anything about horses, but she knew this horse was special to John. If John wanted to be closer to his horse and the country lifestyle he'd left behind, Kayla was the answer. Suddenly, she realized she needed to get over her fear. Her plan would take time and probably a few horseback rides, but John's interest in her house might evaporate for Kayla.

"Will you show me what to do? If I ride?" Stefani stammered, unwilling to believe she was going to get on a horse.

"Of course. And I'll be right beside you. These horses are gentle, so you won't be in any trouble. I promise." His warm grin won her over.

"All right then."

He threw a saddle on a gray horse. "The saddle maintains

your balance, but you'll want to stay above the mount's center of balance. Here." He cupped his hand and Stefani shot up onto the horse. She gripped the nub that he'd called a "pommel" tightly. "Sit up straight. . .shoulders back. That's it. Okay, now you'll want to keep a light, steady hand on the reins. Too tight and you'll hurt the horse. Too loose and you may lose control. Understood?"

Soon Stefani was riding high on a steady gray horse. Next to John's fine mount, her horse looked a bit worn by time and DNA, but Stefani was too tense to care. She felt so high and vulnerable on the huge beast. Every muscle in her body was clenched. John spoke more directions at her, but she was too frightened to take her eyes off the horse's back. She simply nodded quick, short nods.

When she became the slightest bit confident, she clasped the pommel tightly and looked around. The horse trail was incredible with sweeping views of the valley. Huge oaks dotted the path before them and the trail ahead disappeared into a redwood forest. "Stefani, there's a view of the ocean from that ridge up there. Do you want to ride there?"

Stefani's head bobbed up and down swiftly, her jaw so tight she couldn't have answered him with words if she tried. He came beside her and spoke softly, his deep voice coming through loud and clear. "You're doing wonderfully, Stef, I'm so proud of you." She felt herself smile. She was proud of herself, but hearing it from John made her downright giddy. She was actually doing something new, something fresh and exciting, even adventurous.

They continued their slow pace and once at the top of the ridge, John pulled his horse to a halt. Without any command on her part, Stefani's horse stopped as well. John dismounted and allowed his horse to graze. He came to help Stefani down and she went willingly into his upraised arms. Her knees buckled under her and she grabbed tighter to John's muscular frame. "Whoa, my muscles are toast."

"They'll get stronger," he smiled down at her.

Such tranquility was like a dream. She closed her eyes, trying to snap a picture within her mind. There was something magical about being surrounded by his protective arms and quietly overlooking the beautiful ocean view.

"You're a born cowgirl. And here I've been calling you 'princess.' I ought to be ashamed of myself." John winked at her when she finally opened her eyes. "I didn't think you were such an athlete, but you've done so well being on that horse all afternoon."

"I like her." Stefani looked to the horse. "She just knows I have no idea what I'm doing."

John let out a short laugh. "Ah, but you will. You're just a born country gal living in the city." He kept his grip upon her and she didn't even try to break free of it. Her knees were too weak on their own. She snuggled her cheek alongside his chest before pulling away.

"Country girls drive horses and wear boots, I drive a coupe and wear heels. My rubber legs ought to tell you that."

"It's what's in your heart that matters. I think you're a country girl at heart. Those dimples prove it; they've been with us all day. I never see them in the city." He stroked her face with his rugged hand, then bent down with the obvious intention of kissing her, but she broke free of his embrace. She couldn't let *that* happen again. He was toying with her and she was falling for it, hook, line, and sinker.

"I've never seen the ocean from up here and I've lived here all my life," she said brightly as she stared over the ridge, avoiding eye contact.

"Is something the matter, Stefani?"

"No," she replied innocently. She tried to catch her breath and focused intently on the distant ocean. Her plans weren't working at all. She had hoped John would be so enamored with his day that all thoughts of the duplex would dissipate from his head, but instead it was Stefani who couldn't remember where she lived. "I think we should head back. I've got a lot of work to do on the house."

"Fine, Stefani, and you're right. We both have a lot of work to do and I appreciate what a good sport you've been. Come on." He clasped his hands as a makeshift ladder and hoisted her up to her gray mare.

They rode back at a leisurely pace, taking in all the scenery. All too soon, for Stefani's liking, the stables came into view. Without warning, the horse bolted and began trotting at a pace that was beyond her abilities or comfort level. A full gallop soon had Stefani holding onto the reins for dear life.

"He-elp!" she wailed as she bent at the waist and hugged the horse's back and neck. The horse just seemed to go faster, and the tighter she gripped, the quicker the ground seemed to rush past her.

"Pull the reins!" John called after her. She could hear his horse pick up speed and soon he was beside her. "Pull the reins, Stefani!" She wanted to, but then she would have to sit up and she was too afraid to pull away from the comfort of the horse's back. "Stefani. Hang on the reins in your hands and sit up."

Before she had any time to react, they were back at the stables and the horse stopped on its own volition, ending up at the feed bin. Stefani's labored breath and fresh tears couldn't be hidden. Embarrassed, she lashed out. "Thanks for the rescue," she said, haughtily dusting herself off.

He laughed. "Sorry, Stefani, but if you believe you were in any real danger for that forty-yard sprint on that tired old animal, then there's nothing I can say to make you feel any better." He fiddled with his horse's reins and then walked off with both horses into the stables.

Stefani was provoked by his casual attitude. *I might have been killed.* She mumbled continuously under her breath as she walked back to the car. "It wouldn't bother the cowboy; *you* grew up on horses. Riding your fancy, well-trained racehorse, while you leave me to that beast that just wants his oats. This is not a sport; it's just a big, hairy dog that acts on its own wild volition!" John hadn't heard a word of her tirade, but her grumbling soothed her frayed nerves.

five

Stefani hadn't spoken the entire route home from the ranch. She sat stoic, with arms crossed, and let her body language do the talking. John hated to end the day on a sour note. They'd shared such an idyllic time enjoying his favorite thing in the world and he'd seen a glimmer of that side of her she kept so carefully hidden. He wished he hadn't teased her. She'd been an avid horsewoman the whole day. He knew how much she wanted to organize her new home instead of going riding; he should have given her more credit. But it was too late to take it back now.

Monday morning, he watched her from the kitchen window overlooking their shared driveway. She looked the picture of vogue in her sapphire suit; it highlighted her long, shapely legs. She picked up the newspaper, threw him a wicked glance, and got into her car, slamming the door. She was absolutely exasperating, but he was captured regardless. Stefani had an unspoken charm that mystified him.

Remembering her genuine sweetness and those dimples, he knew why. There were the unguarded moments when he'd capture a hint of the woman who had kissed him with genuine passion. It was all the encouragement he needed. Stefani wanted so desperately to hide her emotions; he almost felt sorry for her. He sought the innocent creature who showed herself so rarely, instead of the composed, oftentimes rude persona she hid behind. Stefani pulled out of the driveway in her midnight blue coupe and avoided waving, grimacing at him instead.

John gulped down half a cup of coffee at the kitchen window and tossed the remainder into the sink. His partner honked in the driveway and John grabbed his denim jacket and dashed for the door. His partner, Tom Owens, greeted him. "Hey, I like the new place. Looks kinda fancy for your tastes. You got a new gal you're trying to impress?" Tom leaned toward the steering wheel gazing upward at the Mediterranean home.

"Nah, but I had to spend the money from the sale of the ranch, otherwise I'd give it all to the government. And working for the government, boy, they know just what you've got." They both laughed. "Besides, the only woman I've met here in California who interests me, uh. . .let's just say she's not exactly captivated by my charm. But she does love my house, so I suppose it has its benefits." John smirked.

"So. . .what? You're worried she'll marry you for your house?"

"Ha! No, I'm more worried she'll kill me for it." He laughed again and nodded toward the other half of the duplex. "She lives there; she's my renter." He clicked his tongue. "Cutest thing you ever did see, but, boy, when she sets her mind to something, she has a one-track mind."

"She'll come around."

"Where are we headed today?" John changed the subject. Stefani wasn't just any lady; she was the kind of woman a man thought about marriage for. She was competent, innocent, and needed a good dose of humble pie. John knew just the person to give it to her.

"We're going to Atlas Semiconductors," Tom relayed.

"*The* Atlas Semiconductors?" John asked cautiously.

"The one and only. It's one of our toxic Superfund sites. Last time we were out they had a toxicity plume nearly six thousand feet long and five hundred feet deep." Tom shook his head in disgust. "If they haven't cleaned up their act by now, we're going after them. And nothing would give me greater pleasure." Tom acted like a bounty hunter that would finally get his white whale.

"Atlas is where Stefani, my renter, works," John said slowly, trying to grasp the latest information. He picked up the clipboard containing all the scientific data last gathered, and gasped. "This is pathetic. They've got trichloroethylene levels of twenty-two thousand parts per billion, and look at this, dichloroethylene levels of thirty-eight thousand. Absolute poison. There's no way the drinking water could go unscathed with numbers like these." John reread the figures to make sure he had the numbers right.

"Yeah, and they just keep getting away with it. This time, though, they've got you on the case, John. No one in the EPA has a better reputation than you have for legally bringing these miscreants down. We will have no choice but to act, no matter what the big lobbyists in Washington do. It does my heart proud."

John shook his head in disgust. "Don't have *too* much faith in my abilities. I've just learned to take it slow and catch them by surprise. Their lobbyists just don't have time to act when I'm on the case."

"Welcome to corporate America, John. Just follow the money trail and you'll get to what stinks."

"*This*," he held up the clipboard, "is why I became an environmental scientist. You grow up in a place like Colorado, you just don't want to let big business destroy the land for profit." John was seething; Stefani was working in a poison mill. He knew she had no idea what was going on underneath her. Likely, very few of the employees did.

Suddenly, he felt like a masked avenger. His future report could save Stefani from drinking contaminated coffee from the water cooler or from taking a leisurely stroll along the polluted walkway surrounding her office. He had the distinct pleasure of going after major polluters, but he'd also be there for Stefani. Maybe, just maybe, she might warm up to him if she knew he truly cared for her welfare—if he managed to stop Atlas from poisoning her further.

John and Tom pulled into the corporate driveway with their measuring devices and sterilized tubes for gathering soil and water samples. As they got out of the rented pickup, they were greeted by Atlas's company security. The man in the blue Atlas uniform held up a palm. "No unauthorized vehicles allowed on the property. You'll have to turn around now."

"Environmental Protection Agency," John announced as he held up his badge with conviction. The security man backed away quickly. "We have a report of continued pollutants on the property," John continued, his voice slightly lower to command respect.

"Sorry. Sorry," the officer repeated. He got back into his truck sheepishly and drove off, leaving them to their work. John knew they needed to work quickly. Of course, corporations had no legal right to bother the EPA, but company security could make things more difficult. Partners for only a month, John and Tom had already learned to use their time wisely to get crucial samples. It was such a stupid dance they played, considering that the EPA was there to protect the security guards and others from toxic chemicals, but it was part of the game, nonetheless.

Within ten minutes they had the samples they needed and were off before the security guard returned. If company officials escorted them, the numbers would be decidedly more in the company's favor. The fact was that corporate officials knew where their toxicity plumes were and knew where to steer the EPA away from them, but still keep them on the property. The result was an unrealistic reading. "Let's get back to the lab." John and Tom ran for the truck and squealed out of the parking lot before any of the "officials" could steer them away.

He hoped that after analyzing the samples he would get the opportunity to stop Atlas Semiconductors and, thus, win Stefani's approval. He inhaled, sticking out his chest proudly.

❧

Stefani worked feverishly to get the latest software programs installed for the accounting department. Atlas Semiconductors was having a banner year; no doubt her stock would soon show the reward of her efforts. If she made the kind of money she hoped to, perhaps she could make an outrageous offer to John for the house. The kind he couldn't refuse.

If she could just learn to hold her tongue a little longer, he'd want to give her the desire of her heart. Stefani could turn on the charm if she had to, and for that duplex, she obviously had to. She would prove to her mother that success came to those who worked for it. And she didn't need a man to make her dreams come true.

Amy came running into her office, breathless and flushed. "Stefani, I just saw your landlord out on the running trail!"

Stefani continued to enter her information into the computer in front of her, trying to appear unfazed by Amy's announcement. "Really? I wonder what was he doing there."

"Why are you such a snob? You're worried he's in construction, aren't you? I know how your mind works."

"It's not that I'm a snob, Amy. I just like professional men; it's just my preference. It doesn't make me a snob just because I don't want some urban cowboy as my beau." Stefani bit her lip nervously; no accountant had ever kissed her like John had.

"Suit yourself." Amy slapped her knee, laughing. "Get it? *Suit* yourself. You like businessmen, get it?"

"I get it, Amy. It's just not that funny." Stefani smirked.

"I think you're afraid he might not be interested."

Stefani let out a short laugh. "Amy, when was the last time you saw me worried about what *any* man thought?"

"That's not necessarily something to be proud of, Stefani! When is the last time you had a date? No, wait, a better question. . .when's the last time you had a *second* date?" Amy asked with arms crossed.

Stefani swallowed hard at the question. Amy was right; Stefani wasn't exactly bride material. She always ended up discussing logistics of MIS protocol and boring the guy to death, or saying something she regretted. Added to that, she didn't have the opportunity to meet many men, since most of them worked for her. Her dating life *was* pathetic.

"When was the last time I *wanted* a second date with any of those guys? Look, Amy, I have high standards, I admit that. And most likely, no man will ever live up to them and I'll be an old maid. But better an old maid than to lose everything to a man because of my *feelings*."

"Stefani, listen to you. You sound so hard-hearted. I know you're not that way. I think Mr. Landlord might see through that hard shell of yours, too."

"I kissed him," Stefani said quietly.

"You what?"

"I kissed him. Well, he kissed me. Well, it wasn't so much a kiss as him trying to shut me up. I said something."

"My, what a surprise. You said something?"

"And I also went horseback riding with him. But only because I thought he might want to move because of it," Stefani admitted.

"You know, the frightening thing is, that statement actually makes sense to me. I've been hanging around with you for too long. You thought if you found something he liked, horses, for example, you'd find a reason for him to move. Am I right?"

Stefani crinkled her nose and nodded.

"No offense here, friend. But you're starting to sound like your mother." Amy's words slapped her with the sting of a whip.

"I'm *not* like my mother!"

"Stefani, I know you're not, but you're starting to do things that resemble her greatly. You have a good heart and you love the Lord. But please, stop protecting yourself so much. Getting hurt once in a while helps us grow; it's part of the plan. Have fun with John. Relax. Get to know him; you might find out you like him. Or that men aren't the enemy."

"You don't think I've been hurt enough?"

"Ah, Stef. Pray about it, okay? Listen, the gang from church is going to the Christian music house for coffee tonight. You want to come?"

Stefani was still reeling from the comparison to her mother. "Nah. I would, but I think I'm going to be here late tonight. I have to get this program up and running for accounting."

"Come on, lattes and good music. That new band that performed at church last month is playing. Summer will be over soon and it's going to start getting dark before we leave work; that's so depressing. Let's have some fun while we can. I miss my best friend; it seems like she's always lost in some computer somewhere."

"Thanks, Amy, I appreciate the offer. . .maybe this weekend. I still have unpacking to do and it's my running night."

"Can't you put that schedule of yours aside for one night? It wouldn't kill you. Maybe you could invite John to come with us."

"No! John and I are just acquaintances. Business partners, you might say. The kiss was a fluke. It will never happen again."

"It might if you want it to." Amy smiled.

"Well, I don't want it to."

"I've said my piece, Stefani. I like John and I think he might be good for you. Don't throw him out with the others because of words a dotty old woman told you once."

Stefani felt her throat get tight. "Amy, if I let go of my goal and John disappears like the rest of the men in my life, I've got nothing."

Amy came and sat beside her. "That's not true, Stef. You've always got the Lord and me. I'm not going anywhere. I just wish you'd learn to fly, just a little bit. So let's say, just for the sake of argument, John is just a little fling of a couple dates. Someone you spend time with, go to the movies with, cook for, horseback ride with. . . It's a friendship and friendships grow us, Stefani. Your grandmother was wrong. I know you've heard it a million times from me, but someday maybe you'll have ears for it."

Stefani shook her head. "After my goal is met. If it's meant to be, it will be there after I own the property."

Amy let out a long, deep sigh. "I want to be in your wedding someday. I don't want you to grow old alone just because you missed the boat."

"Oh, Amy, I don't think I'm cut out for marriage." Stefani's chin dropped.

"Nonsense. You're just feeling sorry for yourself."

"No, I'm being realistic. I'm thirty-two years old and all the Christian men out there seem to want some young, sweet thing that hangs on every word they say. Lord knows I don't qualify for *that!* Someday I'll have my grandparents' farmland back and I can enjoy my life *without* a man."

"I'm sure you enjoy your life without a man. My question is, Why would you want to when John Savitch is right next door? If I had a neighbor that looked like him, I wouldn't be so anxious about his moving. If you change your mind about the coffee house, buzz me."

"I will. Have fun tonight and tell the gang I said hi." Stefani smiled widely, thrilled the conversation about John was over. Just the mere mention of his name made her stomach turn over with anxiety. Regardless of her convictions, Stefani was succumbing to the charm of a cowboy. It was getting harder to maintain the cold front when she relished the thought of seeing him at the end of the day.

"I'll tell everyone you said hi." Amy winked and went back to her cubicle.

❧

Stefani arrived home late. John was in the driveway, potting plants in the soil around the perimeter of the peach stamped-concrete walkway. She got out of her car, leaving it in the driveway, and rushed to his side. She stared at the ghastly collection of plants he'd selected, her mouth dangling.

"What are you doing? You're not going to plant those? They don't go with the whole Mediterranean theme of the home." She lifted her arms in expression. "I had pictured queen palms, azaleas, maybe a few crape myrtles. These plants don't match the apricot orchards, they're off center, there's no height to them, you're missing scale. . . I could go on and on." She pointed at the empty plastic containers piled neatly beside his handiwork. "They're. . .they're ugly plants, John," she said plainly.

He smiled. "Welcome home, Stefani. These are drought-resistant plants. Made for the dry, California summers," he stated with conviction. "I won't be accused of using too much precious California water when I use half the commodity as our neighbors." He continued to plant, using his wide, square fingers to press the soil around a sad-looking juniper. "Conservation is key to maintaining God's creation amidst this high population."

Stefani's train of thought disappeared. "What are those awful plastic things in the ground?"

"They're milk jugs." He wiped his brow with the back of his hand and Stefani noticed his hands were covered with mud.

"Why are they in the dirt? Are you trying to get milk from the soil? Or is this some cowboy secret I should know?"

He let out a short laugh. "You fill the jugs with water and turn them over in the dirt. They act as a slow drip system for the plants. No hoses or wasted water necessary," he stated proudly.

"You mean you're going to leave them like that? Not only do I get ugly plants, but I'm supposed to look at garbage, too?" Stefani threw her hand to her hip. "Don't I get some say in the landscaping? It's my home, too, and you're polluting the view with this. . .this garbage."

"It's not garbage. It's recycling and if more people did it, we'd be in a lot better place. Besides, when the plants grow, they'll be hidden." John wiped the dirt from his hands and stood to his full height.

Stefani rolled her eyes. "Well, at least the winters will be garbage free. They will. . .won't they?"

"In the winter, we put funnels in the jugs and catch the

rainwater under the rain gutters." John's eyes sparkled and Stefani got the distinct impression he enjoyed baiting her.

"You're determined to have us be the laughingstock of the neighborhood, aren't you? You actually like the fact that our home looks like it's in the Sahara."

"No, but I'm determined to set a good example for young people that recycling is a way of life."

"We have politically correct plants? Is that what you're telling me? If you knew what this place looked like thirty years ago, you wouldn't be filling it with desert scrub." Stefani turned and walked purposely to her duplex, annoyed such a conversation had even taken place.

"How do you know what this place looked like thirty years ago?" He clapped away the excess dirt from his knees.

Stefani covered her mouth with her hand. How did that slip out? Now she'd lost a bargaining chip; he'd know just how much the house meant to her. The first rule of negotiating was being able to walk away. She recovered after a brief silence. "I can just imagine what it must have been like, that's all. They say it used to be fruit orchards here—everywhere." She started to walk again, but was thwarted by his deep voice.

"Stefani, are you lying? Because you're a terrible liar. Did you know your cheeks turn red when you lie?"

Stefani put her hands to her cheeks and felt their warmth. Her big mouth! She searched his eyes; they seemed to be waiting for an answer. She wasn't lying, really, she just wasn't relaying the whole truth. Suddenly, her conscience kicked in. "Okay, okay. This was my grandparents' farm. I grew up here on this very land in an old clapboard farmhouse that sat about where our duplex is now. Those apricot trees in the back are the last remaining vestige of my family's legacy."

"Your family's all gone?" he asked and she noted the sincere concern in his brow.

"No, they're not *gone*." She shook her head. "They just couldn't afford the taxes on the land anymore. Farming's not a lucrative business here in Silicon Valley. They sold out and moved to Sacramento where it's a little more affordable."

"So why not move to Sacramento yourself?" he asked innocently. "If you miss them so much. It's only two hours away."

"You wouldn't understand."

"Try me."

She considered it, but then retreated. "Let's just say I'm where I belong." She was determined to fulfill the promise she'd made to her grandmother before the loving old woman had gone to be with the Lord. She needed to get the land back in her family. That goal was quickly slipping away because of John Savitch.

John reached out to her, but then pulled his hand back, noticing the dirt. "Do you want to come with me to ride Kayla tonight? We can take old Nelly out for an evening stroll. I bet we could even watch the sunset over the ocean on the ridge. You could tell me about the plants you'd like for the house." His eyes were bright with enthusiasm.

The last thing Stefani wanted was for the bachelor to feel sorry for her. "No, I don't think so. I need to jog tonight. Thanks for the offer, but I still feel like I'm riding Nelly." She rubbed her behind.

"I wish there was something I could say to make things better about the house."

"You could say it's for sale." She was beating a dead horse.

"Stefani, you know owning this house won't change anything."

"That's easy to say when you own it, John. But I suppose I know that deep down," she answered despondently.

He walked closer. "I don't know why God said no, Stefani, but I do know He sees the whole picture." He tried to get her attention, but she ignored him until he used the clean back of his hand to nudge her chin up toward his penetrating green eyes.

"So you've said." She crossed her arms and rolled her eyes. She knew she wasn't going to own the house just yet, but she didn't want to be lectured by the cowboy as to why. Even if he was right, she wasn't ready to admit defeat, especially not to him.

"You don't believe that God is keeping this house from you for a reason."

"I worked hard for my money. I can afford this house and the only thing I see standing in my way is *you*." That wasn't true, but for some reason it felt good to say.

"Then you are misled, Stefani. I'm here for a reason. I own this house and live here for a reason—with *you* as my renter." He pointed his dirt-caked forefinger at her. "I'm not sure what that reason is, but instead of taking your vengeance out on me, why don't you pray? Ask God why He didn't give you this house and wait for His answer. But please leave me out of the loop. It's between you and God. It's not my problem and I'm tired of suffering your wrath."

Stefani felt like she'd been slugged. She hadn't realized just how much her agenda had affected John, but his anger certainly got her attention. The very idea that she had harmed him, in any way, hurt her. It was something her mother would do. *That's exactly what Amy said! Am I becoming like my mother?* She ran into her front door, ending the conversation abruptly.

❧

Days passed and John had stayed mysteriously out of sight. He didn't wave from his kitchen window each morning, he didn't garden in the evening, and he didn't barbecue on his front porch. His absence made Stefani anxious.

Friday evening, the doorbell rang. Stefani was just on her way out to jog, but sighed audibly when she saw John on the porch. For as much as she missed his presence, she wasn't ready to face him yet, either. She turned her back to the door, debating. The last thing she wanted to hear was another lecture on why he owned the house instead of her.

Her guilt played a part in it. She hadn't prayed about it; she'd been too angry. Besides, praying meant doing what John asked of her, and her defiant attitude simply refused to let him control her. John was a man with no emotional attachments to the area or the house. He could afford to go elsewhere and put an end to this whole thing, *so why didn't he?*

She *knew* why of course; people just didn't buy houses and then leave. Home ownership meant permanence and that bothered Stefani to no end. As much as she'd missed John, when she opened the door, her old bulldog self was upon her.

"Yes?" Stefani barked. John was silent; he seemed prepared for her coldness, actually expecting it. Suddenly, he picked her up easily and tossed her over his shoulder like a sack of potatoes. She flailed her arms, bashing him in the back, but she felt like a mere child upon his broad shoulders. "What do you think you're doing? Put me down, you. . .you caveman!"

"Stefani, why can't you just admit we're pretty good together? We have a lot of fun," he explained calmly as he walked toward his side of the duplex. "You're like the second grader who keeps pulling my hair. These running pants look great on you, by the way," he commented and Stefani thought she could actually hear his smile.

"You are such a male chauvinist. Put me down! You throw me a bone like picking out a few plants for the house and I'm supposed to be grateful! Put me down!" she wailed again.

Without further struggle, he placed her gently on her feet in the middle of the driveway and smiled at her smugly. She gave him a look reserved for her most heated arguments, crossing her arms angrily.

"Stefani, would you like to have dinner with me?"

Stefani's mouth dangled aimlessly. "Why do you insist on tormenting me?" She straightened out the legs of her pants. "And why would I want to have dinner with someone that treats me like. . .like a bag of grain?"

"The lady doth protest too much, methinks," he said through a grin.

"What?"

"Shakespeare in *Hamlet*, remember?"

"What on earth are you talking about?"

"Okay, if not Shakespeare, then Dr. Seuss. You don't like green eggs and ham."

"It's been a long time since I read Shakespeare and I don't know Dr. Seuss, so you'll have to refresh my memory if you're trying to make some point." Stefani crossed her arms again, waiting for his answer.

"The guy in Dr. Seuss. He didn't want to eat green eggs and ham at all, remember? But when he *tried* green eggs and ham, he liked them. I think if you'd give this old cowboy a chance and forget this house for five minutes, you'd like me. We had a great time on the horses, and I think we have more in common than you think. We both live in the same place, for example. You just need to get out of those suits more often and into your jeans and relax, that's all. You are a born cowgirl and you'd enjoy it if you'd just let your hair down once in a while."

Stefani instinctively touched her boyish haircut at his comment. Tiny laugh lines were starting to appear next to his eyes and Stefani couldn't remember marveling at anyone being so good-looking. She wanted his house, but right now she wanted him more. She loved his gentle manner and, heaven help her, she may have even liked *him*. But she'd watched her mother toil a lifetime after a lazy father; she wouldn't end up the same way. Why was she being tempted by a handsome day laborer? God knew Stefani needed someone with the same goals she had, didn't He?

"Have dinner with me. Just one dinner." He smiled a lopsided grin and Stefani marveled at the strong line of his chin, oblivious to his question.

six

Stefani stood silent in thought for some time, contemplating the dinner invitation and trying to fight the conflicting feelings welling within her. Lifelong conviction or not, this cowboy was undeniably attractive and the thought of jogging alone versus a quiet dinner with him suddenly paled in importance.

Her answer surprised both of them. "You're right, cowboy, I owe you. Not only will I have dinner with you, I'll *make* you dinner tonight." She shut her door behind her and led him to his house before she had time to change her mind.

"Should I be afraid? You're being awfully nice to me." He pulled her to a stop and she pulled harder to get him walking again.

"I'm a gourmet cook; it's my hobby. Why shouldn't we have dinner together tonight?" *It doesn't mean anything*, she added silently.

"Yes, why not? But, should I be afraid? You're not going to poison me or anything, right?" John's eyes narrowed suspiciously.

"I've just decided to be more neighborly. That's all. This is your house and this is my way of acknowledging that fact. No strings attached, no ulterior motives, and no hidden agenda. You've told me you'll sell to me if and when the time comes and I'm satisfied with that." *For now.*

"What should we have for dinner? Should I go to the grocery store?" he asked as they entered his kitchen. He rubbed his hands together in eagerness.

"That depends. What do you have in the fridge?" Stefani opened his refrigerator without an invitation and riffled through the contents. She came up with potatoes, an onion, a chicken breast, and two soft drinks. "This is it?" She held up the contents.

"I haven't shopped."

"Since when, 1958?" She giggled and held his hand to show she didn't mean any harm. "I'm teasing. We'll have a fine dinner. There's some fresh rosemary growing wild in the back; do you have flour?"

"I do!" he answered, his eyes wide in enthusiasm.

"Then I have an idea."

Again, John tried to start the stove and the burner burst into a small flame. Stefani jumped back and John immediately tossed baking soda on the element to put out the fire. He leaned on the counter and looked closely at the stove. "No wonder. There's a small leak right here."

Stefani remembered how uncivil she'd been when the stove caught on fire the first time. She'd just assumed John was inept. It never occurred to her the brand-new stove may not have been installed correctly.

"Let's go to my house. The stove works fine there. Until you get that thing fixed, I'd say it's off-limits, but judging by your refrigerator contents, that shouldn't be a problem," Stefani suggested.

"We'll go to your place on one condition. You said you could make a dinner out of those ingredients and that's all you can use. You've got me intrigued. Considering that's what I usually have around the house, I might be able to learn something useful."

"Deal," she grinned.

Stefani whipped up a simple but elegant meal of Italian gnocchi in rosemary and olive oil, topped with grilled chicken. John moaned with pleasure at each bite. "This is fabulous. How'd a city girl like you learn how to cook like this?"

"I wasn't always a city girl, John. Remember, this used to be an orchard and my Italian grandparents used gnocchi as a staple. Gnocchi is so cheap to make and it feeds so many, it's the Italian rice. Just equal parts flour and potatoes and a perfect starchy pasta is yours for pennies. Now, of course, it's a gourmet delicacy in the Italian trattorias, but we with Italian heritage know better. We also know what it does to our waistlines." She patted her tummy, then reached for the dishes to clear them.

John took the floral patterned dishes from her hands and stood before her. Stefani froze, fearing the magnetism between them. He must have sensed her discomfort because he pulled away. "You never cease to surprise me, Stefani. Thank you for dinner."

Stefani turned from him and looked into the bottom of her stainless steel sink. She needed to just get this over with, to apologize and be done with John for good. "John, I'm sorry I've been so rude." She tried to explain her actions, though she knew they didn't excuse her behavior. "I have always worked with this one goal in mind, that this property would be in my family again. That *I* would be the one to make enough to pay the taxes and take care of the remaining orchard trees. Even if the orchard is long gone and there are just a few trees. I don't expect you to understand, but I'm a very determined person."

"No kidding."

"When it didn't happen according to my plan, I just didn't know what God wanted me to do with this life. I took it out on you and I'm sorry." She looked over her shoulder into his eyes, which seemed to understand.

"Stefani, you are forgiven. Thank you for telling me and thank you for dinner. I'd better be going."

So soon? "You're welcome."

"I'm glad to hear you prayed about the situation," he said calmly. Stefani fidgeted uncomfortably. She hadn't prayed about the house, and she was still seething even if she was able to control her outward emotions. Her face flushed red. "Are you busy tomorrow night?" he asked.

"Saturday night? Uh, no. Did you want me to cook again?"

"Well, I would, but I'd rather treat you to a restaurant. It will give you a break and return the kind favor of this beautiful dinner."

"John, I don't know."

"I just want to bring you to dinner and then to see Kayla in the rodeo," he explained. "No strings attached, as you say. Just two friends getting together for a good rodeo."

"You're in the rodeo?" she asked incredulously.

"No, *I'm* not. Kayla, my horse, is; she's performing in the barrel race tomorrow night. The women do the barrel racing; that's what Kayla's been trained for and she's very good at it. I'd love for you to see what you could do on a horse, eventually."

"I have no idea what barrel racing is, so maybe you should find somebody else. Somebody who would appreciate the rodeo. I wouldn't want to waste the ticket. I'm still a city girl at heart, remember?" she offered as an excuse. She wanted to spare his feelings, because there was no way anything could develop from this relationship. Stefani had watched her mother toil a lifetime for the handsome man she loved. Stefani would never fall for someone who wasn't as driven as her.

"Oh, come on, Stefani, you said you had nothing else to do. And I don't want somebody else to come with me. I want *you,*" he said directly.

Stefani forgot to breathe for a moment as she stared into the depth of his green eyes. His statement, although meant to be purely innocuous, was filled with a passion that caused her blood to heat. "What does one *wear* to a rodeo?"

He grinned knowingly at her. "I think you can probably guess that a dream date with me would include jeans and a pair of boots. The French restaurant was a fluke and it probably won't be repeated too soon. I prefer ordering in English. Meat loaf and potatoes."

"A date? This is a date? I thought you said it was two friends getting together."

"Well, yes, two friends on a date. Unless you have some

type of rule against dating your landlord."

"No, I, uh. . .no. Jeans and a pair of boots. Got it." *Oh, how do I get myself into these situations?*

"Thank you for the dinner," he whispered in a low growl, coming toward her with the wall that made up his chest. Stefani tried to react, to steel herself against his obvious intention, but it was of little use, she wanted his kiss desperately. She closed her eyes and prepared for it, but he left a small peck on her cheek and said good night. By the time she realized what had happened and opened her eyes, she was watching his back. The door slammed and she jumped.

❧

Stefani spent her Saturday morning shopping for a pair of boots and trying to ignore the high school thrill she felt about her upcoming date. It was just two friends, she kept telling herself. She checked all the department stores and couldn't find a pair of boots. Clearly, it was a fad that had seen its day. She didn't want to stand out as a city girl, so she looked up western wear in the phone book. Shock registered when she found there was such a store in the high-tech Silicon Valley. She clambered into her car and dashed to the store, still questioning the effort for a man who had stolen her heart's desire and life's goal in one fell swoop.

She crinkled her nose at the tacky storefront when she arrived. The walls were lined with barn-type, rough-planked wood, and boots in every color and style imaginable hung from every nook and cranny. "I can't believe I'm doing this." She ran her hand through her hair, tempted to walk back out and forget this ridiculous charade. John liked a woman in boots; it was the least she could do for this one night. After that, she'd let him know she was only interested in a business relationship with him. When he wanted to sell the house, fine. Otherwise, she was strictly his tenant.

A salesman approached her wearing what appeared to be painted-on jeans hugging his too-thin frame. He topped it with an oversized cowboy hat, which might have tipped him over from the sheer weight of it. "May I help you, ma'am?" he asked, tipping his hat. Stefani looked around her, wondering if she was still in California. She felt like she'd just stepped into Texas. Or at least what she thought might be Texas since she'd never been there.

"I'm looking for a pair of boots," she stated, followed by a long sigh.

"Fer ridin', fer dancin', fer what?" he asked.

"Uh, I don't know. Wearing, I guess." She bit her lower lip. "No, wait, for riding," she clarified.

"Right this way, little lady."

The salesman personified all the preconceived ideas she'd formed about cowboys: not too bright, poor dressers, and living in a time no longer present. *This is definitely a mistake.*

"We've got ostrich or alligator boots; does that interest you?" He tipped his hat again. "They are all the rage this year."

"Yes, I saw them lined up all over town," Stefani snapped.

"Beg yer pardon?"

"Nothing." Stefani couldn't help her grimace. "Just regular leather, cow leather," she clarified. "Cow leather would be just fine. Thanks." She forced a smile. The salesman held out an arm and motioned to a chair near the corner. She took her leather loafer off and the salesman helped her from the seat.

"You'll want to stand for your fitting," he informed her.

"Of course," she nodded and stood.

He brought a bevy of boxes down from the wall. Stefani worried this was going to take all day. She checked her watch and sucked in a deep breath. "Don't worry," the salesman smiled, noting her apprehension. "Once we get you started, it won't take long. Now the instep will feel tight at first and that's what you want, because once it's worn in, you won't ever want to take them off. They'll feel like a second skin." His drawl magically disappeared.

Stefani tried on quite a few pairs before deciding on a white and light beige suede combination. She couldn't imagine where she'd ever wear them again, but she nodded at the salesman. "These are fine. I like them," she stated, as much to convince herself as the salesman.

"Would you like to wear them now?" he asked.

"Uh, no, just wrap them, that'll be fine."

She heard the cash register ring and the salesman smiled. "That will be one hundred sixty-three dollars and fifty cents," he said cheerfully.

"One hundred—" she began in disbelief and then snapped her mouth shut.

"These are genuine buckskin, lined—"

She held up a palm. "Spare me the details, that's all Greek to me, anyway." She handed her debit card over with reserve. This was going to be an expensive date. In the parking lot, she hoped that John's rider for Kayla wore the same sized shoe. "I hope someone will get some use out of these things," she muttered to herself as she threw the bag into her car.

Stefani dressed in her jeans and a linen shirt in a cocoa color that complemented her new boots perfectly. She sized herself up in the mirror, turning to get each angle. As much as she hated to admit it, the boots looked good. They emphasized the length of her legs and made her figure look quite pleasing. If she'd only bought a hat to cover up her lack of hair, she'd be set.

Her crisp, ironed shirt was probably missing some fringe or something, but for a first attempt, Stefani thought she might actually blend in at the rodeo. The doorbell rang and Stefani felt the butterflies in her stomach flutter into her chest.

It had been a long time since she'd had a date. And this was the first one she'd been excited about since. . .she couldn't remember when. She opened the door and nearly swooned at the sight of John. He wore a black shirt and his standard jeans with scuffed black boots. He was rugged and beautiful all at the same time. Stefani felt herself smile shyly, embarrassed he might read her thoughts.

"Stefani, you look absolutely gorgeous." John's eyes rested on her boots. "I am so honored you'd put a pair of boots on for me. They look like they were made for you."

"At this price, they should have been," Stefani said sarcastically, then bit her lip, praying for God's help in holding her tongue. There was a thin line between being herself and being offensive. Stefani vowed to try to be sweet for one night.

John's gaze lingered on her boots then came to her eyes. "Well, whatever they cost, they were worth it," he confided, while nodding his head. He held out his hand and Stefani took it readily. "My lady, your chariot awaits."

Stefani climbed into the SUV and inhaled the rich smell of leather mixed with John's lingering scent of musk cologne. It was a magical combination that sent her head spinning. John stepped in and turned on the ignition, a calming classical CD played, and Stefani looked at John questioningly. *Who is this man?* At first, she'd sized him up as some hick, but there were things about her first assessment that conflicted deeply. First of all, why had he chosen to live in the city? And how did he afford the expensive duplex, car, and horse, but still wear a workingman's clothes to work? And finally, the one that hit her the hardest: Why did it matter what he did for a living? She loved being with him, loved the way he stood up for himself, and loved the way he seemed to take control, even with Stefani's independent personality.

"Stefani, everything okay? You look a little lost."

"Everything's fine. I was just thinking about work. I'm excited about the rodeo. It's my first," she added, as though she needed to relay such information.

"I think you'll like it. It's not for the faint of heart and I have a feeling that you'll stand up to it." He winked and backed out of the driveway.

Stefani could only take his comment as a compliment. After a quiet dinner in a small coffee shop, they arrived at the large Cow Palace where the event would take place. An air of excitement emanated from the parking lot. Huge pickups filled the lot and giant searchlights crisscrossed in the night sky, announcing the big event.

John took her hand and Stefani felt princess-like, as though she belonged in a fairy tale. Clearly, he was handsomer than any cowboy she'd seen and she felt proud to be on his arm. They entered the Cow Palace and the air was thick with a dry, brown dust making visibility difficult. The stench from the animals nearly bowled Stefani over and suddenly, the romance of the magical night dissipated with the overwhelming smell.

She covered her nose with her hand and tried to be as discreet as possible.

"You'll get used to it," John announced, yelling over the loud whoops of the crowd and the booming sound system.

"I don't want to get used to it; this is awful. They need a big spray can of air freshener or something."

John's expression dropped. "Are you saying you don't want to stay?"

"No, no, I don't want to leave." She grasped his hand tighter and her eyes said she was sorry. She'd bite her tongue if she had to, but she was going to enjoy this night. Calf roping was taking place in the ring and dust flew as men on horses dashed from a gate and worked together to surround a calf and rope it. Stefani had seen the looped rope on television, but she would have never believed it was real. She found herself yelling in her excitement and watching the timed scores with anticipation. "Go! Get him! Faster!" she shouted, surprising herself. She'd crinkle her eyes shut, peering through one barely opened eye as each calf fell, and then she'd holler like a coyote.

John sat up straight in his seat when the barrel riding started. "This is Kayla's event. Justine Hastings is the rider. Oh, Lord, let her do well," he muttered. His excitement was obvious; his green eyes had a sparkle in them she'd never seen. He was like a kid who had just gotten his first bike. "Here comes the first rider!"

After a loud horn, a horse raced into the arena at full speed and headed directly for one of three barrels in the ring. The racer rode a cloverleaf pattern around the barrels, getting so close she actually tottered two of the barrels, but none of them fell over and John said that was a successful ride. Stefani held her breath until each rider finished, fretting over each barrel. Her hands were in tight fists from the suspense.

When Kayla's turn to ride came, Stefani lost interest in the horse and instead focused on the beautiful blond who rode her. Her hair was long and unlike the other riders; she didn't have it tightened or clasped. It just fell luxuriously around her shoulders. Stefani watched John's expression, looking for some sign of his attraction for the young, avid horsewoman; but John's eyes never left Kayla. His fists were tightened and he said nothing. On the third barrel, Kayla dropped the barrel and Stefani felt guilty she wasn't upset at the failure. Justine was disqualified. "I'm sorry, John." Stefani touched his arm and he clasped her hand in his own.

"Thanks, Stefani. Kayla's young; it's not her time yet. I didn't expect much more than this," John emphasized. "Justine gets too excited still. She's got to learn not to cut it so tightly and stay calm."

"The rider looks pretty upset about dropping the barrels," Stefani commented, hoping he'd give her an indication of who Justine was to him.

"She ought to be. She rode lazy. She knows better. Well, it's her reputation at stake."

"Reputation? She looked like she was going pretty fast; dropping a barrel could happen to anyone."

"You've got to be more than fast in the barrel race. She knows that. It's precision." He looked at her and she felt his eyes warm her to the core. His expression changed. His intense green eyes and his strong jawline were all that existed. "May I kiss you, Stefani?"

She only nodded her response and he placed a soft, warm kiss on her lips. Not enough to be offensive in a crowd, just enough to make her realize she was falling in love with this cowboy. It probably wasn't the last time she'd wear those boots.

seven

John got called to work first thing Sunday morning. The lab readings he'd done on Stefani's company were at an all-time high toxicity level. It was time to make his move. Atlas Semiconductors was going to pay this time. John paced within his kitchen; he felt like such a traitor. What would Stefani say when she knew her company wasn't business as usual? These things took time, but there was no doubt in his mind: The Silicon Valley site of Atlas Semiconductors was going to be shut down—perhaps permanently. How on earth was he going to tell Stefani what he did for a living? It was bad enough he'd taken the house she so desired. Now, her job might be in jeopardy as well. He sighed. Had he known the toxicity was that high, he would have told Stefani right away. But she'd thought he was a country bumpkin, and he enjoyed baiting her for her own pride. Now, the joke was on him.

Stefani knocked on the back door wearing a lovely sapphire blue dress to match her eyes and a smile as wide as could be. Their evening at the rodeo had been a pleasant one, and she had obviously enjoyed it as much as he had. The sparkle in her eyes said it all.

"Good morning, John," she whispered coquettishly, clearly putting her harsh nature behind them. John relished the sight of her childish dimples in full view, knowing she finally trusted him. He cringed, acknowledging he'd let her down again. The house seemed like a non-issue for her now, but what would she do when she found out about her job? "Have you ever seen a more perfect day to worship?"

"Good morning, sunshine. Did you sleep well?"

"I did," she answered dreamily and John was tempted right

then and there to take her in his arms. But he couldn't; he needed to make his intentions clear and his occupation known. "Ready for church?" she asked.

"Actually, I can't go today, Stefani. I got called in to work on an emergency, so it seems I won't make it. But say a prayer for me, okay?" *I'm going to need it.*

Stefani's eyes fell to the floor and her dimples faded. "Yeah, sure."

"Stefani, this has nothing to do with you. I have to work today. Something very important came up."

"Do you get paid overtime to work on Sunday?" she asked innocently.

"No, it's just something I have to do every now and then."

"Okay, so I'll see you later tonight."

"I'm looking forward to it." He closed the door slowly and beat himself up for misleading her. He should have told her he wasn't building some structure over the weekend. Should have told her he was an environmental scientist who had serious business. *Lord, how can I be so deceitful? Leading her to believe I'm some simple cowboy straight from the ranch. Instead of the man who may put her out of work. . .*

He watched her walk despondently to her car and wave good-bye. He smiled and returned the wave and got into his SUV. Once at the lab, John rubbed his throbbing temples over the data before him. Beginning procedures for shutting down a company was tedious work, riddled with facts and lawyer speak. He set about getting all the paperwork ready for the law to take over and came home tired and annoyed.

He cupped his hand over the back of his strained neck and walked into his back door when he heard a small voice call him from outside the garage door. "John?"

He looked outside and saw the redheaded woman from Stefani's church who had flirted with him. She held a brown grocery bag and a ready smile. Her head was downcast and her big green eyes blinked exaggeratedly. "Are you looking for Stefani?" he asked.

"No, actually, I was looking for you. You didn't come to church today and I thought maybe you hadn't been properly welcomed into the church. I brought dinner to make," she said confidently. "I'm Rachel. Rachel Cummings, remember?" she added in her light tone. "Stefani's friend?"

"Sure, I remember." *Just what I need.*

"I told Stefani I'd come by tonight. She said you like home-cooked meals, so I thought I might help out. I guess you had to work all day."

John had a pretty good idea Rachel's landing on his doorstep was her own doing, not Stefani's, but he didn't know how to remedy the situation without calling her a liar.

"I have to feed my horse tonight," he offered by way of excuse. He clicked his tongue as though that was it. His answer.

"You have a horse?" she continued.

"A buckskin mare," he answered proudly. "She's a barrel racer and it's my night to brush her down and make sure the ranch fed her properly. So I really appreciate the offer, but—"

"I'd love to see her," she replied hastily. "I love horses. Is there somewhere I can put this stuff down?" She lifted a perfectly manicured hand from the grocery bag and tossed her long red curls. Although she wore jeans and a simple tailored T-shirt, her makeup was more fitting for a night out at a dance club. Bright red lipstick dotted her light complexion and her eyelashes were as black as night.

John hesitated before answering, looking to Stefani's front door to see if she might come out and rescue him. "Sure, come on in." He led her to the kitchen and she began putting the groceries away as though she knew where everything went.

"I hope you like steak and mushrooms," she said happily.

"Rachel, I'm a little pressed for time. I've been working all day and I've got to get to Kayla, my horse, before sundown."

"We've got plenty of time before the sun goes down. Did you want me to start dinner first or did you want to take me to see Kayla first?"

John couldn't stand pushy women. Independent, self-assured, confident, that was all fine, but pushy was just annoying. And with the mood he was in, he didn't have much patience. "Look, Rachel—"

"Oh, look, there's Stefani." Rachel pointed out the kitchen window to where Stefani stood in the driveway in her running pants, breathing hard.

Stefani checked her watch and turned off her timer, then bent over resting her hands upon her knees to catch her breath after her nightly run. John watched her do the same thing every evening and it invigorated him. Her tiny, shapely frame stopped in exactly the same spot every night, so oblivious to everything around her except the familiarity of her routine. She was beautiful, even fresh from an athletic sprint, her short haircut delightfully coifed in a sweatband. It was messy and darling all at once.

John closed his eyes momentarily when Stefani turned. He watched with agony as Stefani's smile disappeared when she noticed Rachel Cummings in his kitchen. He felt the instant loss of trust that he'd worked so hard for. Why had he allowed this conniving beauty to come between him and the woman he wanted? He didn't deserve the trust anyway, at least not until he told her the truth about his job. This was probably his just desserts.

"I better go say hi; I'll be right back." Rachel bounced outside and John followed slowly. He splayed his hand against the door frame and tried to show Stefani he was innocent. "Stefani. Oh, Stefani, hi!" Rachel called.

"Hi, Rachel, how are you?"

"I'm fine. You look pretty worn out. Is it really necessary for you to get all sweaty like that to keep skinny? What a shame."

John's teeth clenched. "Stefani's in fantastic shape. The one time I ran with her, I had trouble keeping up," he offered, hoping to quell a rising flame.

"Now, John, I can't believe that," Rachel purred, then directed her attention back to Stefani. "John and I are having dinner. Then he's taking me to see his horse, Kayla."

John's eyes fell shut again. "Rachel stopped by when I got home from work." *Uninvited,* he added silently.

"That's great. Well, you two enjoy yourselves." Stefani walked toward her duplex and gave a quick glance over her shoulder.

"Rachel, will you excuse me?"

"John, I—no, fine, you go ahead, I'll get dinner started."

"You know what? I'm really sorry, but Stefani and I had plans for tonight. So if you don't mind, I'd just as soon we not do dinner tonight."

"But—"

"Look, I don't want to be rude, but I had plans tonight."

"Well, maybe we could reschedule," she offered with honeyed sweetness.

Just then, Stefani's garage door opened and she backed out in her sporty coupe. She had all the windows rolled down and her still glistening face was weary from her run. She failed to look at either of them and squealed out of the driveway, offering a wave from her window.

"Well, whatever your plans are, it looks like they're canceled. Now, I won't take no for an answer, John. It's my Christian duty to make sure you're welcomed into our church. I'd do it for anybody."

John walked into the kitchen and grappled with the ingredients Rachel had strewn about in his kitchen. "I'm flattered, really I am," he paused, handing her the grocery bag, "but—"

"I bought these steaks and they shouldn't go to waste. They were expensive. Let me just cook them for you. You can feed your horse alone if it makes you feel better. Far be it from me to intrude."

John finally relented, wondering how he would ever make Stefani believe he didn't invite every beautiful woman to meet Kayla. "Fine. Why don't you hand me the lettuce? I'll make the salad," he offered, worrying idle hands would only make his precarious situation worse. The faster this ended, the better.

Rachel tried in vain to appear like she knew what she was doing in the kitchen. It was obvious she spent very little time at the stove and she kept smiling that exasperating grin when she thought he might be on to her game. "It's been so long since I grilled a steak," she said after opening the oven door and plumes of smoke came billowing out. Since he'd had it repaired, he knew that the billows of smoke had nothing to do with the stove.

John's eyebrows lifted and he nodded, "Are these mushrooms for the salad?"

"No, I'm going to sauté them. Do you have any olive oil?" she asked.

"I do, just bought it yesterday." John reached up into the cupboard and brought down an enormous bottle of extra virgin olive oil, one that would probably last him a lifetime, if such things kept. "Stefani says you shouldn't be without this stuff."

"And she's right. It's a cook's best friend," Rachel answered knowingly.

Then I imagine you two are casual acquaintances, John thought through his smile. Rachel took the bottle from him and poured half the contents into a frying pan while John snapped his awed mouth shut. After a quick rinse in the sink, she dropped the full-sized mushroom caps into the pan. The poor vegetables floated wildly amidst the excess oil. As the contents began to heat and sputter, tiny drops of oil splattered everywhere in the kitchen and the mushrooms twisted and writhed in their greasy death.

John watched Rachel bite her lip nervously when she added onions and the grease droplets increased. "Ouch!" she yelped. He turned the burner down and looked at her hand, which was red from the fresh hot grease burning her thumb.

"Here, put some ice on that. I'll finish the vegetables." He got out a coffee can from under the sink and poured the excess oil into it. Then he finished with the vegetables, while Rachel sat on a nearby kitchen stool. Despite his efforts, any vitamins or minerals had been drowned out by the olive oil and it still looked anything but appetizing.

"I'm sorry, I don't know what's come over me," Rachel whined apologetically as she held her thumb under a bag of ice. "Nervous maybe."

John smiled, feeling sorry for Rachel. She was clearly trying to impress him and although he wasn't the least bit interested, it was no reason to be rude. It was a fine line between encouraging her affections and treating her compassionately.

When dinner was finally on the table, only the oil dripping from the mushrooms moistened the charred steak. "Dear Lord, we thank You for Rachel's special effort on the meal and ask for Your blessing upon it and the hands that prepared it. In Jesus' Name. Amen." John took his first bite, while Rachel watched expectantly. He smiled while he chewed, and chewed and chewed some more.

"How is it?" she asked.

"Well-done, just like I like it," he lied, hoping to spare her feelings. Thinking back to Stefani's gourmet meal from potatoes and flour, John couldn't help but compare the terrible meal made with the grocer's finest ingredients. It wasn't the cooking; it was simply the fact that Stefani was so accomplished, so competent in all she set her mind to. No wonder it bothered her so much to lose the house. Everything she had worked for, Stefani had accomplished with the exception of the duplex. His duplex.

Rachel left all the dishes piled on the sink because her thumb hurt too much when she dropped it into the hot water. John didn't care; he was just thankful his politeness could come to an end. "Well, I really appreciate dinner, but as I've said, I've got to get to Kayla, my horse."

"Of course; we had a deal." She stopped in the doorway, expectantly.

"Well, thanks again." Just then Stefani whizzed into the driveway. She glared at them both and drove into her garage, shutting the great door behind her.

"Good night," John said without further delay and jogged to Stefani's doorstep. He rang continuously until she finally answered. "Stefani, before you go getting angry with me, you should know I've never seen Rachel before or since you introduced us at church. Her coming over here was her idea and I had no idea she'd be here."

"I know." Stefani shrugged. "Come on in." She opened the door wider.

"What do you mean, you know?" John put a fist to his hip and glared.

"She does that for all the new men at church. She wants first dibs on them, I suppose. So you want to come in?" she asked casually.

"Stefani, if you knew all this, why didn't you warn me? Why didn't you stick around and show her we are—"

"Yes, we are what, John?"

He ignored her question. "So if you weren't jealous, where did you go before taking time to shower?" He looked down at her, his eyebrows lowered in expectation.

"I had to rush to the drug store. I thought you might be needing these." She held up a roll of antacids and turned to run down the hallway, giggling like a child all the way.

"Oh, no, you don't. Get back here!" He chased after her and caught her in the dining room doorway. Catching her up in an embrace, the laughter suddenly died and her natural beauty silenced him. Her blue eyes shone with delight and her full dimples slowly disappeared, revealing that she was as caught in the moment as he was. Her skin was flawless and her gentle, full lips a natural pink.

"Don't, John. Come on, I need a shower." She pretended to struggle, but she never left his arms and his grasp inexplicably tightened.

How could he do this? He was falling in love with her and

when she found out he'd taken her house *and* her job away. . . Soon, there would be no sweet dimples, no laughter, and worst of all, no trust in her sparkling blue eyes. *Why didn't I tell her what I do for a living before it was too late?*

"I've got to go feed Kayla," he said abruptly and turned, leaving her and her confused expression alone.

eight

Stefani finally fell to her knees in prayer. *What is happening to me?* She was falling for John, regardless of what he did for a living. All the preparation and nagging her mother had given her were pointless against how John made her *feel*. Although she'd tried many times, she just couldn't bring herself to ask him what he did for a job. *Am I such a snob that I can't handle the answer?*

She looked to the heavens, praying for an answer. "Dear Lord, John is everything I thought I ever wanted in a man. Sweet-tempered, godly, self-sufficient, but, Lord, I don't want to repeat the sins of my mother. He's too handsome, Lord, he's not a businessman, and he works with his hands. He's everything my grandmother warned me about. I promised my grandmother, Lord. I promised her I wouldn't let a man come before my goal. I'm waiting on the house, Lord, but please, help me see Your plan in this. Help me focus on my goal and not on John Savitch. This house should belong to me, but I *have* to do it alone. It's what I promised my grandmother. Give me the strength, Lord!"

As if things weren't bad enough, Stefani's mother was coming to visit. She groaned aloud at the thought. Stefani hadn't explained she was living on the old family orchard. What would her mother say when she saw the beautiful Mediterranean duplex that had replaced the old clapboard farmhouse? The land Stefani had vowed to own, in the hands of the handsome John Savitch. She cringed. Although her mother didn't know about Stefani's vow to her grandmother, Stefani still felt like a failure and somehow she knew her mother would point that out. Her mother would arrive with some sort of agenda. Gladys *never* visited her daughter without invoking some type of crisis. Stefani braced for it, whatever it was this time.

The doorbell rang and Stefani combed her hair nervously with her fingers and instinctively straightened her back. "Mom!" She took her mother into an embrace and her mother stiffened at the show of affection. She pulled away quickly.

"That church allows you enough money to live in a place like this." Gladys let out a small snort.

"Mother, the church doesn't require any money from me. The Bible asks that I tithe ten percent to Him. Since God has allowed me all this, how could I *not* give a mere ten percent?" Stefani changed the subject. "Do you want to see the house?"

"I'm seeing it, ain't I?" Gladys Lencioni set her bags in the foyer with a thunder. "First, you change your name to my parents' name! Lencioni ain't good enough for you, then you buy this monstrosity from the enemy. It's just like you, you always was too good for us."

"Mom, we had to sell the house because the taxes were too high. The man who bought it was very nice, he had nothing to do with our woes."

"You don't remember. You were too young and you always did look at things through rose-colored glasses instead of how they really are."

"Come see the rest of the house, Mom." Stefani wanted to clarify she was only renting, but what good would that do with her mother's bias so blatant.

"Child, we had a simple life, never had need of any of this fancy housing or a new name! Of course, you were right about my spelling, Stefani. Schooling wasn't important on the orchard, but you could have changed that to the right spelling and I wouldn't have cared."

Sure, she says that now. Gladys's small but robust body wandered into each room, letting out a short, annoyed sigh with each sight. "You always did think you were above your roots. We buy you an education and you leave us high and dry."

"Mother, the name Willems is just easier for me at work. People have an easier time with it. It's not a reflection on you or Dad. Well, what do you think of me living on Nana and Papa Willems' old orchard? Isn't it neat how the family stayed on the land?" Stefani asked enthusiastically. "Like we were pioneers or something and it's our destiny."

"Except they didn't stay on the land. We sold the land and now look at it with all these fancy new townhouses nobody can afford. Can't make an honest wage anymore. No, you have to build computers and stuff nobody has need of. You grow quality food like apricots and they throw you off the land."

"Mama, they didn't throw you off the land until it stopped producing fruit and we couldn't pay the taxes." *And it wouldn't have stopped if Dad had worked the land.*

"There were years of fruit left in them trees. Life just got too complicated around here."

"Mama, I made homemade ravioli for dinner." Stefani hoped a well-made dinner might change her mother's attitude, but she remained doubtful. "I invited my landlord for dinner. John Savitch is his name. He's a cowboy and he owns a beautiful horse that's in the rodeo." She felt like she was talking to a sulking child.

"How does a cowboy make a living here? You're gonna support him, too? Him and that church of yours? Seems like you're going to have to make more and more money. Your father always took care of his family."

Since when? "Mama, John owns this house. He makes a decent living, I promise. And we're just friends, so please don't go asking him about grandchildren, all right?"

Her mother grumbled something under her breath, and Stefani carried her mother's bags upstairs and into the guest room. Once there, she leaned against the door frame and stifled her tears. *How am I ever going to get through these two weeks?*

The doorbell broke into her thoughts and she silently thanked God for John's availability for dinner. It would take off a little of the pressure of being with her mother alone. Her dad usually came along and helped curtail her mother's nagging, but Dad hadn't been able to come this time. Stefani had to wonder why and prayed it wasn't her mother's dramatic pause before she announced some big news. Gladys rarely came to town, but when she did it was either to nag Stefani about a husband or announce some distant relative had died. Stefani and Amy had jokingly called her mother the grim reaper since Gladys's appearance usually meant someone's death.

Stefani raced down the steps and her eyes lit up at the sight of John. His cowboy gear was gone and he wore his gorgeous navy suit and carried two bouquets of yellow roses. "I can smell that dinner from my place. I probably would have showed up with or without an invitation."

"It's portabella mushroom and sun-dried tomato ravioli." Stefani smiled at him.

Stefani's mother glared from around the kitchen entryway, sizing John up without any thought of decorum or discretion.

"Mrs. Willems?"

"Lencioni. Mrs. Lencioni. Stefani's too good for our name," she answered bitterly.

Stefani gave a nervous grin. "Come on in, John. Dinner will be ready soon. This is my mother, Gladys Lencioni. Mom, this is John Savitch."

"I thought you were a cowboy," Gladys replied suspiciously.

"I am. Would you like to see my registration card with the American Quarter Horse Association?" He grabbed for his wallet and Stefani bit back her smile.

"I have to stir the sauce." Stefani lifted her eyebrows at John, wishing him luck. John may handle a thousand pounds of horseflesh with ease, but he had yet to meet her mother.

"You didn't add enough basil and you got too much marjoram in it," Gladys barked as she walked past her. "I can smell it. Doesn't smell right."

John cut Gladys off. "Did you teach Stefani to cook, Mrs. Lencioni? She's unrivaled around these parts. She cooks for the church members when they have babies and bakes cakes for the neighbors. She's very popular around here," he said proudly.

"My mama taught me that a way to a man's heart was through his stomach. But never met a man who'd eat this fancy stuff Stefani dishes up. Stefani's papa likes meat in his ravioli, none of this fancy whatever-you-call-it she sticks in there. Beef. What's wrong with simple beef?"

"I like everything Stefani cooks." John threw her a knowing smile, and suddenly, Stefani was sorry she'd involved him in this fiasco. There was no pleasing her mother and she pitied John for his futile attempts. She whisked the sauce too violently, trying to ignore the conversation around her.

"If you like this, then you ain't never had a proper meat and potatoes meal made for you." Gladys put a hand to her wide hips. "I'll make you *dinner* one night."

John was unswayed. "My mama used to fry us up big, aged steaks on the ranch. One for my dad, my sister, and me. Mmm, mmm, that was living. She'd cover it in onions and fresh-ground pepper; I thought I'd never taste the likes of it again. Then, Stefani made us steaks one night after riding horses and I couldn't remember what Ma's ever tasted like." He put an arm around Stefani while she chopped cucumbers for the salad. Stefani thought she'd fall into him, his strength was so comforting. Every part of her was tensed and nervous, but his solid arm helped her relax—helped her remember her mother's visit was only temporary.

Gladys harrumphed. She walked past Stefani and added spices to the sauce, physically moving Stefani out of her way. "She still can't make her grandmother's sauce right."

"Mrs. Lencioni, it was good of you to teach Stefani to cook. A lot of women her age have no idea what to do in the kitchen. I can certainly testify to that," he mumbled and Stefani grinned.

Gladys stopped stirring the sauce and looked at John, first warily, then happily. "Well, thank you, young man. It's nice to be appreciated that way. Has Stefani made her gnocchi for you yet? All the farmers' wives used to try to duplicate our gnocchi, but they could never get the consistency right. I believe Stefani could do that in her sleep. She's a right quick learner when she sets her mind to something."

Stefani was stunned. It was the first nice thing Stefani could ever remember her mother saying about her. "She *has* made her gnocchi and do you know, I'd never heard of it," John said with a special kind of stupid in his answer. He was playing the village idiot and her mother was relishing it. *Oh, I love him.* She loved him! The thought startled her, but at the same time, she knew it might be true. She was falling for John Savitch and she didn't want him to ever move from her life. No matter what her grandmother said.

"Shall we eat?" Stefani asked abruptly, hoping to change her train of thought.

"Of course. Mrs. Lencioni, you sit at the head of the table here." John pulled out her chair and placed the linen napkin across her lap as she sat down. "Stefani's guest of honor should sit in the place of honor."

"Call me Gladys, John. I'm not that old," she smiled broadly at him and Stefani just shook her head. No wonder she'd fallen for John. If he could work his wiles on Gladys Lencioni, Stefani was powerless against him.

"Gladys, I would love for you to come out tomorrow morning after church and see my horse. Kayla is going to be a champion barrel racer some day. It's the perfect time for you to see her because she is dappling right now." John sat down next to Gladys and looked intently into the older woman's eyes. Stefani felt invisible for a moment, but she knew John was just trying to keep her mother's attention off of her.

"Dappling?" Gladys asked.

"Yes, she's a buckskin mare. She has this wonderful deer-like coat. It's a beautiful golden brown color; you've never seen anything like it. She has black socks and a black mane and tail. In the summer, her coat lightens and she gets these beautiful blond spots on her golden coat. She's just one of the prettiest horses you've ever seen."

"Church? You go to church, young man?" Gladys asked, her eyes thinning. Not a mention of the fact they'd been discussing horses.

"Uh-huh. I go to Stefani's church. Why do you ask?" John asked nonchalantly.

"And you own this duplex?" she asked rudely, her pudgy hand resting, once again, on her hip.

"I don't understand. What does going to church have to do with my house?" John looked to Stefani questioningly.

"My mother thinks that the church is just after our money. She doesn't believe in God," Stefani stated plainly.

"Oh, Gladys, no. Really?" John asked with the utmost sincerity and melancholy in his voice.

For a moment, Stefani thought her mother actually looked uncomfortable and she felt the tiniest bit of compassion. Something Stefani thought she had lost long ago.

"God never did anything for my family. We struggled with this land and we had to sell it—if there is a God, He just watched it happen." Gladys looked straight at John, challenging him to give her an answer. Stefani had gotten into this same argument many a time and never arrived at an understanding. Her mother's heart was hardened. Hardened and bitter.

Still, John persisted. "Gladys, God doesn't promise us an easy life. He promises to take care of our needs. You've never wanted for anything." John studied her mother and Stefani waited with bated breath hoping her mother wouldn't lash out, her usual reaction.

"No thanks to that God of yours. I'm surprised such a bright young man would believe in God. Did you go to college? You know Stefani went to Stanford, earned her own scholarships and everything."

"Stefani, I didn't know that. How wonderful. Well, you see

right there, Gladys, God's done a pretty good job of looking after Stefani since you and Mr. Lencioni left the area. And Stefani's had the finest education available. I think if God was going to dupe someone, it wouldn't be a smart cookie like your daughter."

"Stefani can take care of herself. She always has been like that. Very independent and determined and smart as a whip. The teachers used to rave about her when she was a child."

Stefani sat down slowly, unable to finish serving. She had never heard her mother say something positive about her, and John had gotten her to say almost nothing but since he arrived. Still, it was probably just her way of avoiding the subject of God.

"I know, Stefani is very intelligent." John put his hand on Stefani's and she tried to still her trembling fingers.

John sensed her nervousness and picked up the serving spoon and began placing portions on each plate. "Salad, Gladys?"

"Please," she answered politely.

"You know Stefani almost bought this house. That's how we met." John filled up their iced tea glasses and sat back down.

"Stefani couldn't afford this house," she declared with a laugh. *That* was the mother she knew.

"Of course she could, Gladys. Stefani has one of the highest paying jobs in Silicon Valley. She's an MIS manager," he said confidently.

"Is that why you're interested in her?" Gladys remarked. Stefani's breath left her. She could take no more.

"Excuse me." Stefani screeched her chair as she got up. She tossed her linen napkin carelessly on the table.

Stefani scrambled up the stairs and quietly shut her bedroom door behind her. She flopped onto her green wrought iron bed and cried into her floral pillow. *Why did I say yes when Mother asked to visit?* She knew it could only spell trouble. Stefani had only just learned she was in love with

John Savitch and her mother would destroy that, too.

Stefani's love for the rugged cowboy would go unrequited, just like her feelings for all her past boyfriends had. Once Gladys Lencioni showed them what a loser Stefani was underneath her confident business persona, they were gone. Run off by her mother's callous portrayal of Stefani. Fearful that Stefani might turn out like her mother. And now, John would be next. Stefani would not only lose his friendship, but her home as well. She had known better than to get involved with a good-looking cowboy. It was her own fault.

Stefani tried to pull herself together and go back downstairs, but every time she lifted herself from the bed, she just flopped back down again. Broken. *How can I explain my absence to John?* Leaving was the worst course of action. *Why couldn't I just have held it together a little longer?* She didn't want to face John again. He'd probably made a fast exit anyway. Excuses were common responses to Gladys Lencioni's biting personality.

The longer she waited, the worse the situation seemed. She felt trapped in her own home. A small knock sounded on her door and Stefani wiped away her tears with the back of her hand. She sucked in a deep breath and prepared to meet her mother.

Opening the door, she saw John and the tenderness in his green eyes softened her immediately. "Your dinner's getting cold," he said gently.

Stefani dropped her face into her hands. "I can't go back down there, John. She hates me. I'm sorry I left you with her, but I just didn't know what else to do. I'm surprised you're even still here. Usually, people meet my mother and run the other direction."

"Stefani." He took her by the hand and placed her on the settee by the window where he then sat next to her. "There is nothing your mother could say that would change my feelings for you. I'm falling in love with you, Stefani Willems or Lencioni, whatever your name is."

Stefani closed her eyes and listened to the words ring again and again in her ears. She dropped her head onto John's shoulder and cuddled herself next to his collarbone where she could hear the steady beat of his heart. It was quick and steady and so very comforting.

"Your mom has agreed to apologize. Why don't you come downstairs and eat that beautiful dessert you made? My mouth has been watering all through dinner. Come on, I'll make the coffee."

"I'm sor—"

"None of that. It's all over. Let's go downstairs and eat that dessert. I promised I'd take your mom to see Kayla while you're in church tomorrow morning."

"John, you didn't have to do that. I can stay home from church tomorrow. You've done more than enough."

"No, I think it will be good for you to get your worship time in while she's here. I invited your mom to church with us, but she's afraid they'll take her wallet, I think." He let out a short laugh and stood, holding out his hand to help her up. "Come on, let's get downstairs before my reputation is ruined. I'm not usually inclined to invite myself into ladies' bedrooms."

"Well, I'm glad to hear that." Stefani stood and John pulled her close.

"But while we do have a little privacy, I might as well take advantage of it." He kissed her while he held her jaw in his hands. His grasp was firm and gentle and his kiss held definite intention. Stefani felt herself shiver, but it was over too soon and he let her go. "Okay. That's enough of that. *This* is not a good idea." He pulled her out of her room by the hand and they descended the staircase together. "I think there might be kryptonite in there; I suddenly feel weak," he joked.

"Thank you, John."

He smiled, then his voice echoed through the home, "Gladys, slice the tiramisu, the chef has returned."

"Stefani makes the best tiramisu you ever had, John.

Learned it from her grandmother and she makes it the real way, soaked in espresso with genuine marscapone cheese, none of these cheap imitations they use in the Italian restaurants today. That stuff just tastes like cheap whipped cream." Gladys took John by the arm. "Now you just sit down and take a load off. Tall man like yourself needs a break after a long day."

Stefani knew that was the closest she would come to an apology from her mother, but it was enough. John had put out yet another fire, but Stefani was still mortified that he'd witnessed Gladys's behavior at its finest. Still, the evening would go on and Stefani had managed to come out of her room without tears. *Blessed Heavenly Father, thank You for this man,* she thought as she watched him with her mother. He had her mother laughing and telling stories of the old neighborhood while Stefani watched with both awe and delight.

He was truly gifted with charm and incredible good looks. She sat wondering how it was that he was still single at his age. What dark secret did he harbor that kept the women at bay?

He was falling in love with *her*—plain Stefani Willems. She played his words over and over again in her head after he'd gone home. She touched her bedroom wall, knowing he was just on the other side of it. "John, I think I love you," she whispered to the wall while she ran her fingers lightly down its surface. "And I don't care if you dig ditches for a living. It doesn't matter."

Stefani fell asleep with a smile on her face as she dreamed of the man with those sea green eyes and the rugged physique. Not one thought of her mother crept into her precious dreams.

nine

"He'll never marry you if that's what you're thinking," Stefani's mom quipped as she tackled the kitchen counter with a sponge. "Men like John don't marry; they just play with hearts. You need to find yourself a nice little accountant and settle down. I've been waiting a long time for grandchildren and if you wait much longer, there won't be any."

The sun shone brightly into the kitchen, canceling out the darkness and doom Stefani's mother seemed to predict. "Mother, I'm thirty-two and I have a good job and a nice house; I'm not thinking about marriage. Can't you just be happy for me?"

"That's what all unmarried women say," Gladys continued. "That, and they're just waiting for the right man to come along. Humph."

"Mom, you didn't marry until you were thirty-four and in that day, you were considered middle-aged. You've heard the old adage, 'Marry in haste, repent at leisure,' " Stefani shot back, embarrassed by her rising temper.

"I had plenty of opportunities to marry earlier, missy. I know men, my dear. I lived with your father for thirty-five years! And while John Savitch is as charming and handsome as they come, he's not the type that marries. He has too many interests as it is. There's that horse of his, which, while it is beautiful, I have to admit I don't get the infatuation. It's just a big dog that eats him out of house and home. And who know what he does for a job? A man that charming doesn't work hard for a living, that's for sure. It's probably something illegal."

"Mother! That's enough. John would never do something illegal. He's a good, Christian man." Stefani bit her lip nervously, as was her habit whenever she got defensive. Although she trusted John, she really was starting to wonder about his profession. She knew he made good money, but she was no closer to finding out what he did every day. She thought about asking him, but it seemed to her that if he had wanted to tell her, he would have done so by now. And she had to admit, she hadn't exactly made it easy for him with all her rude "cowboy" comments. *No. I won't let my mother's paranoia get to me. I don't need to second-guess everything just because my mother told me to.*

Her mother continued, trying to goad her into questioning John. "The churchgoing ones are the ones you have to watch out for. Sinners on Saturday night, in the front pew Sunday morning." Gladys shook her head and Stefani just rolled her eyes.

"Mom, what is it you have against the church? You haven't been in one for twenty-five years, so I fail to see how you know all about it."

"Don't you talk to me that way, young lady. I know all about the church." She stopped scrubbing and wagged a stubby finger at Stefani. Gladys began nodding her head continuously while she talked. "This young woman used to live right on the corner over there. Well, her husband used to beat her every day with a stick. And do you know that woman went to church like clockwork every morning. Every morning, she'd cart her two kids up the street so she could listen to some preacher tell her to come back home and be a good, submissive wife. All the church is about is male dominance. Male dominance and money."

"Mother, that is ridiculous."

"You tell that to Fanny Reilly." Gladys pointed again then threw her sponge into the sink. "That poor woman went to that preacher and told him about her husband. Told him that man of hers drank and hit her with a stick. And do you know what that preacher told her?"

"I can't imagine," Stefani answered, rolling her eyes again.

"He told her to go home and be a good wife, then he'd stop

drinking and everything would be okay. 'Divorce is wrong,' he'd say and then let that poor family go back and get beaten again. Don't you tell me I don't know about the church. I know all I want to know."

"Mother, they didn't understand alcoholism back then like they do now. And you can't blame the church for people's sins. People *sin*, Mom. It's a fact of life, and it has been since Eve held out that apple for Adam to bite into."

"I lived a right fine life, young lady. You can't call me a sinner. You mind your manners."

"Mother, everyone's a sinner. If you ever thought evil about someone, you're a sinner. If you ever said the Lord's name in vain, you're a sinner. And you've done that three times since breakfast! If you ever dishonored your parents or Dad's parents, you're a sinner. How can you tell me such baloney?"

"Well, I still say that boy won't marry you," Gladys snapped back. It was her favorite ploy. If she was losing a battle, she just changed the subject.

"Mom, I have everything I want now," Stefani explained. "Do you know I am the highest paid female at my company?"

"Well, I still don't have any grandchildren."

"That's what *you* want, Mom."

"Of course I want that. It's my time in life to spoil a grandbaby. Since you're an only child, that leaves little room for somebody else to make me a grandma."

Stefani couldn't imagine. Gladys Lencioni had never spoiled anything in her life, except maybe a jar of apricots one season. The thought of a poor, helpless baby against her mother infuriated Stefani. If she ever did have a baby, she didn't want it near Gladys Lencioni. She would protect that baby with everything she had. Her baby would never believe that if she didn't grow up to be perfect, she wasn't worthy. Her baby would be loved. Loved like no other. She'd never allow her child into that unhealthy atmosphere without her protection.

What am I thinking? Yes, John had said he may be falling in love with her, but that could have been as a Christian brother trying to help her when she was in need. Stefani didn't know his intentions and she had learned early in life that relying on others for happiness would only lead to pain. You have to make your own happiness.

"Mother, could we please change the subject? I'm not having any babies. It requires a husband, something you will notice I don't have."

"Fine," she said shortly. "So what are we doing today? I've been milling about this big house all week by myself. I'm ready to get out. You know three of our original apricot trees are still there? They needed a good pruning and a little tender care, but I took care of it today."

"Mom, you shouldn't wear yourself out. John thought you might enjoy a stroll across the Golden Gate Bridge today. Do you think you're up for it?"

"With all the foreigners? I don't think so."

"Mom, John planned a special day for us in San Francisco. It would mean a lot to me if you went without complaining."

"Complain? When do *I* complain?"

"Complain is probably too strong of a word. Mom, let's just try to enjoy ourselves today. We'll have a nice crab lunch on the wharf and act like tourists ourselves, okay?"

"Your Uncle Louie used to crack crabs for a living. Wasn't a soul that was faster. *Snap, snap, snap* and the whole crab right there on your plate ready to eat." Gladys snapped her fingers. "Not so much as a shell in sight."

John's SUV roared with anticipation and Gladys stepped up into the front seat. Stefani had to admit how thankful she was for John's nearly constant companionship during her mother's visit. Without it, she didn't know how long she would have lasted without losing her temper with her mother. But, so far, she had managed to pray through all the little quips and underhanded remarks effectively and hadn't said anything she regretted.

"Is there a reason this truck has to be so far off the ground?

Nearly breaks my hip to get into it. You know us older folks don't have the strong bones you young people have. Fragile. That's what they are after a lifetime of living. Fragile. Someday you'll find out."

"Do you need some help getting in? It's a four-wheel drive, Mrs. Lencioni; it has to be high off the ground to get through the snow and the mud."

"It doesn't snow here," she answered flatly.

"I'm from Colorado and it does snow there. Besides, I'll head up to Tahoe as much as possible to ski this winter."

Gladys turned around and faced Stefani in the backseat. "So he's a *skier,* too. You sure seem to have a lot of free time on your hands and a lot of hobbies. My husband never did have time for hobbies, didn't have time to play with a big animal like a horse. When we had a horse, it worked for its dinner, just like we had to."

John sounded defensive for the first time. "Kayla has the potential to earn upwards of hundreds of thousands when she gets strong. She's from excellent lineage and her days as a champion barrel racer are close. I'll recover my expenses, don't you worry."

"I'm not worried. Fine man like yourself obviously has the ability to make money *somehow,*" she said, her voice tinged with insinuation.

"Stefani, where do you want to go first, the wharf or the Golden Gate Bridge?"

"The fog has cleared already; let's go to the bridge. We'll have a nice, brisk walk. Hopefully, we'll get there before all the tour buses."

"Perfect idea," John replied.

John parked in the lot near the famous San Francisco landmark, and the trio became silent as they took in the view. There wasn't a cloud in the sky, a rarity in the city by the bay. The magnificent brick red suspension bridge was a monument to man's accomplishments. Its peaks were well in the air, their brilliant orange highlighted against the clear sky.

The sparkling blue ocean glimmered with hope against the backdrop of magnificent mountains. Stefani couldn't imagine a more magnificent view.

"It's breathtaking," Stefani sighed. "Mom, have you ever done this?"

"In all my years on the orchard, I never did this. We just never had time," Gladys remarked. "If there's one thing I always wanted to do in this lifetime it was walk across that incredible bridge," she said so wistfully that Stefani watched her curiously. It wasn't like her mother to say such dreamy things. Stefani smiled in satisfaction.

"Too bad Dad can't join us. This is going to be a day to remember."

"Well, you know your father. He's probably got three different morning papers spread out all over the living room with a Western playing loud on the TV. He'd view this as foolishness. Just wasted energy."

"I don't know, Mom; he might like it. There's nothing like being a tourist in your hometown. It adds an air of excitement being with all those people seeing it for the first time."

"Well, let's see if I can get across it and maybe next time your father will join us."

The threesome gathered at the opening of the bridge and were nearly bowled over by the strong winds. The brisk, chilly sea breeze from the Pacific Ocean prompted them all to go back and get their coats. They started again and Stefani thrilled at the grin her mother wore for the entire span of the bridge. Even when the older woman started to breathe heavily, she never let out a complaint or a gripe.

Tourists were everywhere, snapping pictures and speaking in several languages. Stefani took out her own camera and told her mother and John to pose. They both wore big smiles while they said "cheese," and then Stefani traded places and they each shot her picture with the other. Once they reached the other side, Gladys was weary and her smile was beginning to fade.

"Gladys, why don't you let me run back and get the car," John suggested.

"No, no. I can do it," she answered breathlessly.

"Mom, we know you can do it. John is just probably thinking of your stamina for the whole day. We still want to have lunch on the wharf and maybe a little shopping. We just don't want you to use up all your energy so early in the day."

"Very well, you don't have to twist my arm. I'll sit and wait." They found a bench at the park and sat down. "I'm an old woman, there's no shame in that."

John waved them a farewell and started a slow sprint back across the bridge. Stefani crossed her arms while she enjoyed the view, taking in all the sailboats and huge tankers that filled the busy bay. She couldn't think of a thing to say to her mother, so she just watched the boats and the people walking in the park.

"Stefani?"

"Yeah, Mom?"

"Stefani, there's something I want to tell you."

Oh, no. Who died? "What is it, Mom?" Stefani pried her eyes from the tourists and looked at her mother. Her face was haggard and pale, not the robust woman Stefani remembered growing up with. Although Gladys had been here a week, as Stefani looked at her mother under the bright sunlight she realized it was the first time she had *really* looked at her. Her mom was getting on in years, but Stefani hadn't noticed how old she looked this visit.

"Stefani, I'm really proud of you."

Stefani waited for the other shoe to fall and crush her in the process. "Mom, what brought this on?" Stefani was uncomfortable. This newfound appreciation of Stefani was eerie and frightening. And obviously not what Gladys had to say.

"Stefani, there's no easy way to say this, so I'm just going to blurt it out. I have cancer."

"Mom, no!" Stefani felt herself go white as the blood drained from her face. A sick feeling covered her. Of all the reasons. . . Stefani would have never guessed her mother's health. Gladys simply seemed too mean to ever get sick. Illness seemed to hold no power over her. Stefani checked her attitude, finally comprehending the scope of what she'd been told. For once, her mother's crisis was genuine. "Mom, so are you in chemotherapy? Radiation? What?"

"I'm not doing any of that stuff." Gladys let her hand cut through the air sharply.

"Why, Mom? Did they say it was inoperable?"

"Stefani, those doctors just tear you up with all their poisons and machines. I don't want to go that way. I would just as soon go peacefully. I'm not going to fight it. If death comes, I'm prepared to meet it."

Stefani softened for the first time since her mother's visit. Gladys wouldn't fight because she had no hope. And she had no hope because she didn't have Jesus. Stefani said a silent prayer. "Good, Mom, don't fight it, that's just what the devil would want you to do. He'd want you to give up. Just submit to him and go willingly."

"Stefani Lencioni, don't you talk to me that way. I ain't going to no devil and none of your religious talk is gonna convince me otherwise. I lived a good life, Miss Willems! I took care of your father like a good wife should and I always saw that you were raised right. I found the money to pay for your housing so you could go to Stanford. My daughter! You went to Stanford University because your father and me sacrificed. We saved and scrimped so you'd have a better life than we did. So don't go spouting your *going to the devil* garbage at me."

Stefani closed her eyes in prayer right there. Again. What could she possibly tell her mother? Gladys was closed to anything Stefani had to say and she'd go to her deathbed the martyr she wanted to be. Unless God intervened. *Please, God. I can't think of anything else to pray. Please.*

Stefani knew she needed to love her mother—to free herself of the anger and judgment she clung to and just love her mother. Not just be polite and roll her eyes behind her back, but truly *love* her mother. . .to see her through God's eyes: as a broken child, hurting and victimized by a harsh world.

"Mom, I want you to fight the cancer. Tell me what the doctor told you."

"He said I probably have ovarian cancer, but he can't be sure until he cuts me open. I've been having a lot of stomach problems, not able to keep food down. . . I thought it was indigestion."

Ovarian cancer. It sounded so ominous, so deadly.

"Mom, I'll come stay with you. I want you to have the surgery."

"Why?" Gladys crossed her arms. "There's no guarantees."

Stefani called on God for the next words. "Because I love you, Mom, and I want you to live as long as possible. I want you to know how much God loves you. How much I love you," she choked out.

Gladys said nothing, but she was deep in thought. Stefani took that as a positive sign. When they arrived at Fisherman's Wharf with nary a word, John watched them both suspiciously. He told innocent cowboy stories of his days on the ranch. It was lighthearted and unimportant, but it broke the silence and kept their minds occupied.

ten

John breathed a sigh of relief. Stefani's mother had finally left. Gladys brought out a side of Stefani that John would not have believed existed. Stefani second-guessed her every decision, bit her nails nervously, and, worst of all, kept her precious dimples hidden completely. If there ever was a smile, it was counterfeit. Nothing was good enough for Gladys Lencioni. After two weeks of watching Stefani suffer, trying to live up to sheer perfection, John was ready to send Gladys home via parcel post.

Something had snapped in Stefani after their day in San Francisco. He didn't know what had caused it and she wouldn't discuss it. But something had definitely jolted her security. The spunk and fire that made her "Stefani" was gone. He should have been awed by her uncanny self-control, by her ability to bite her tongue, even when Gladys purposely baited her, but he was sobered by her behavior. He wondered where his feisty beloved had disappeared to.

"Well, she's gone," John said from their driveway as he waved good-bye to Gladys.

"But her legacy remains," Stefani said cryptically as she turned to her side of the duplex. "I'll see you on Saturday night. Is that still okay?"

"I wouldn't miss it for the world. I'm honored you asked me."

"Wear your suit, please?"

"Stefani, I won't embarrass you," John said evenly. She smiled. He traced her dimples gently, thrilled for the chance to touch her again. To see her dimples and that smile that lit up his world. . .

"I know you won't. I can't believe I ever thought that you would."

John hadn't told Stefani about his profession. She had been so preoccupied with Gladys, the time never seemed right. Still, guilt prevailed. John had been working away on the legal means to get Atlas Semiconductor shut down. The courts worked slowly and he wished he could tell Stefani without endangering his building case against Atlas. He tried to remind himself he was acting in her best interest. Any information she had could be held against her in future motions. The more naive she was, the safer her job would be in the future.

The days were shorter now as were their evening rides on Kayla and Nelly. As Stefani's company celebrated its record earnings, John promised to attend the party as her date.

John dressed in a black tuxedo and straightened the bow tie. It was too tight for his neck and he fiddled with it, trying to loosen it. Staring at his reflection he paused. *I must be in love. I didn't think any woman could get me into a monkey suit without the occasion of my wedding.* But here he stood, wildly uncomfortable in his tux and dress shoes—all for the occasion of Atlas Semiconductors' success. The irony of attending a prosperity event for one of the Silicon Valley's largest polluters was not lost on the environmental scientist.

He picked up the pale pink roses from his countertop and pulled his car out into the driveway. He rang Stefani's bell and when she opened the door, his legs felt weak at the sight of her. "Stefani, you are absolutely stunning. These flowers would hardly do you justice." He held up the bouquet and smiled.

Her dimples appeared in full and her rosy cheeks were luminous against her long, soft pink gown, which had an empire waist and no sleeves. She wore long white gloves and a sapphire pendant that was the exact color and shimmer of her eyes. Her hair had quickly grown out to make her appear more feminine. The bob she now wore was both stylish and businesslike. Now that her natural beauty wasn't hindered by the severe haircut, her dimples looked more at home on her sweet face.

"Thank you; I hope I don't get seasick," Stefani answered the compliment. "You look—let's just say I'm honored you would lose the boots for a night."

John held up a hand. "Enough said. I'm blushing. Shall we?"

Stefani took his outstretched hand and he handed her the bouquet. He felt like he was reliving his prom as he watched her gently arrange the flowers in a vase of water. Only tonight he didn't have to borrow his mom's car, and his date was far more attractive. They spoke easily as they drove to the port of San Francisco, laughing and thoroughly enjoying one another's company. It was just like getting together with a best friend; they easily fell into step together. John felt like a wolf in sheep's clothing, entering the den of the enemy.

Atlas Semiconductors' grand extravaganza was nothing more than an expensive ploy. A scheme to show the world, and especially the stockholders, all was well. John knew the truth. And by tonight, so would Stefani. He promised himself, work ethics aside, that he couldn't deceive the woman he loved any longer.

Once at the covered dock, they lined up among the revelers in their black ties and evening gowns. An air of excitement emanated from the crowd and within minutes they were boarding the private luxury liner for an elegant tour of the San Francisco Bay. A loud horn sounded and they were off, cruising the rugged surf of Bay waters. The city lights were magical. As they went under the Bay Bridge, the clock tower onshore rang out to them like a beacon in the night. John felt hope. Stefani would understand his dilemma, he reasoned. *She had to.*

"Look at the Golden Gate Bridge tonight. Your mother would love this view," John commented. Stefani bit her lip again. *What's going on with Stefani?* She seemed so on edge.

"Yes, she would, wouldn't she?" Stefani replied sadly. She changed her tone immediately, plunging into a new topic. "*This* is heaven on earth." Stefani cuddled her back into his arms as they leaned on the railing, taking in all the sights. The great triangle-shaped skyscraper was the centerpiece of the city, and the tallest, a nearby building, was lit up like a Christmas tree. "I can breathe the air of Union Square and just see the interior of my favorite stores decorated for the holidays," she giggled.

"Stefani, that's sea air, not shopping air," he chastised.

"Whatever. I bet you can't buy boots like mine in San Francisco, though."

"If you could buy them here, *you'd* find them," John quipped, wrapping his arms around her waist even tighter. "My little shopper."

Suddenly, she turned to face him, childlike delight in her face. "Don't you love the soothing feeling of the boat rocking? I feel like a baby being rocked to sleep with your gentle arms wrapped around me."

"Honestly? No, it makes me a little ill." He turned her back around and she nestled into his chest.

"Oh, come on, big cowboy like yourself. Former rodeo star—I've seen all your trophies in the living room and I think riding a bucking bull has to be a little harsh on one's stomach. This is nothing; quit being a baby."

"You don't have time to be sick on a bull; it's over before the fear subsides enough to get sick to your stomach. Then you just have to worry about getting out of the way!" He cuddled her just the slightest bit tighter, thrilled to be with the woman of his dreams. *Alone*. Although he still preferred her in boots along the peninsula ridge, he was happy to share in her corporate world tonight. To see another side of her which she'd kept compartmentalized in her ordered world.

Stefani shrugged. "So I have a guy question. Why do men save their trophies? I mean, a guy could get a trophy in the third grade for a spelling bee and it still holds a place of honor in his house. Why is that?"

John threw back his head in laughter. "I don't know, Stefani. I don't know."

"But it's true, isn't it? It's some kind of rite of passage we women just don't get. I mean, I got a trophy for figure skating in the sixth grade, but I don't have any idea where it is. But you know where all yours are, I'd be willing to bet. It's true, right?"

"I suppose it is, my dear."

"I saw your rodeo trophies next to the *floral couch*."

"Are you making fun of my sofa again?"

"*Moi?* Never! I'm appalled you would ask such a thing. After all, if you want to keep something that might be mistaken for garbage in your house, that is completely your business. I suppose you'll get married someday and all those trophies will slowly disappear."

"A dire prediction, Miss Willems."

"What's dire? The idea of getting rid of your trophies or getting married?"

"The trophies, of course. I think I'd make a right fine husband." *As soon as you accept my proposal.*

The captain soon announced that dinner would be served shortly and the party goers milled about toward the tables. The boat turned at the Golden Gate Bridge and took a tour of the inlet near Tiburon, an expensive tourist area in the north bay, then back to the San Francisco side once again. John and Stefani found their way to the table with their placards and enjoyed an expensive Italian water together.

"We're sitting at the head table?" John crinkled his nose distastefully.

"It's reserved for executives and board members; that's us." Stefan shrugged.

John became decidedly more uncomfortable, hoping he wouldn't be recognized. It wasn't that he had a problem facing these wicked men, who put profit before people, but doing so on Stefani's arm made him feel like an absolute heel. He certainly didn't want Stefani held accountable for his actions. An environmental scientist working for the Environmental Protection Agency was no friend of big business. And certainly no friend to Atlas Semiconductors. If he didn't act soon, he'd be no friend to Stefani as well.

"I ordered you a steak," Stefani whispered as they sat down.

"Oh." John sounded disappointed.

"I thought you loved steaks. It was either that or salmon and you just didn't seem like the salmon type to me. Do they have salmon in Colorado?"

"Yes, Stefani, we have salmon. You just forget I've had a Stefani's grilled steak and onions. Certainly, no San Francisco chef could ever duplicate such a feast." He winked at her.

"I don't know, you've had Rachel Cummings' steak, too." She let out a small giggle. John was reminded of the unappetizing charred beef, made by the church flirt. "I'm sorry, that was rude." Her dimples soon appeared again, showing she had no real remorse.

"No comment, but I think I'll take one of those antacids if you have one. Suddenly I don't feel so well." The combination of the swaying of the boat and not being able to see the shore from his seated position made John too aware of his motion sickness.

Suddenly, John noticed the security guard that John and Tom had encountered when they collected soil and water samples. John instantly became self-conscious, wondering how he might avoid the man, but at six-foot-two, seated at the head table with the company's beautiful MIS manager, he doubted he could remain unseen for long. Hopefully, enough time had passed and he wouldn't be recognized.

"Miss Willems, I'm glad you could make it." A stern voice broke into John's fears and he forced his eyes from the security guard.

"Hello, Mr. Travers," Stefani replied professionally, then she turned to John. He eyed the older man carefully. There was something about the distinguished looking gentleman John didn't like. Something eerily familiar. . . "Mr. Travers, I'd like you to meet my friend. This is John Savitch."

"Pleasure to meet you, young man. Savitch, that sounds familiar. What do you do with yourself during the day?"

Stefani stared at him expectantly as John remained speechless. He still hadn't told Stefani what he did for a living yet.

And now just didn't seem like the time.

"Mr. Travers is the CEO and president of Atlas Semiconductors," Stefani explained, trying to break the uncomfortable silence, as well as let John know that this was her boss. John didn't need the prodding or the explanation; he knew all about Mr. Travers. He could tell by the condescending attitude, the air of eliteness, and the smug smile.

"Is that so, Mr. Travers. CEO?" John answered. *Travers.* The man responsible for a toxicity plume that seeped five hundred feet into the ground. . . The man who knowingly allowed his employees to dump toxic waste with the expressed arrogance he wouldn't get caught. . . Or at least held accountable. What was the most frustrating about the man's name was the fact that it wasn't the first time John had run across it. John had closed down another plant in Colorado that bore Travers' name on the CEO plate. He prayed Travers wouldn't recognize him. Not yet anyway.

"It takes patience and drive to achieve success in this Silicon Valley," Mr. Travers boasted. "If you're going to court our little Stefani here, you're going to have to have some of that drive. She's quite a go-getter. She has what it takes." He winked.

"I invest in rodeo horses," John blurted without lying. Of course he did invest in Kayla, but it was hardly a profitable business. Yet.

"Interesting. Is there much of a market for that type of thing around here?" The CEO lifted his glass and John's stomach turned at the stench of the strong, golden amber liquid.

"Not really," John said coolly.

The CEO had had enough of John's small talk. *Thank goodness.* Then, Travers' eyes flickered and narrowed. "John Savitch," he said slowly with malice. "John Savitch, from Colorado? Stefani Willems, have you lost your mind?"

"Wh-what?" Stefani stuttered.

Travers whispered through gritted teeth. "I'm going upstairs and I'm telling the captain to stop this boat. You and your date, Miss Willems, will exit without incident or you'll be looking for a new job come Monday. Do you understand?"

"Well, no, I don't," Stefani answered with the sweetest inflection of innocence. John felt like the worst type of heel.

"I knew I'd seen that face before. Stefani, you get this. . .this *gentleman* off my boat immediately, do you understand me?"

She looked at the plank floor. Travers disappeared and it wasn't long before they felt the boat turn. "Maybe we'd better go up on deck," John suggested.

"What on earth is going on?" Stefani pleaded. "John, how do you and Mr. Travers know one another?"

"Let's just get off the boat. I'll explain it all to you when we're away from all these investors. No sense upsetting Mr. Travers any more than we already have."

"We? I didn't do a thing. It seemed to be *you* that upset him," Stefani remarked quietly.

The boat soon came to a sudden halt and the couple could hear the roar of the crowd inside as they worried over the dinner cruise suddenly stopping. Mr. Travers saw to their exit personally, his big, burly security guard alongside him. Stefani's blue eyes were wide with fright as they were dropped on a cold, dark, abandoned pier in the middle of the San Francisco night. The Bay Bridge stood looming above them, the noise of the traffic silenced by the howling ocean winds that swept through the Golden Gate, leaving their bitter, moist chill with the lone couple.

John watched Stefani with a sense of wonder. She was so beautiful in her sleek, pale pink gown. Sophisticated and pure, all at the same time. Her blue eyes were awash with confusion and she fingered the back of her long, elegant neck self-consciously. Her beauty made his knees feel weak. Things were about to change and he dreaded it.

Stefani Willems did not trust people easily. She had trusted him and before he knew it, that trust had evaporated. Gone like the elegance of the night. They stood on the filthy pier, John in his tuxedo and Stefani in her designer gown with the smell of tar and diesel overwhelming their senses. Suddenly, Stefani reached out, her pink satin wrap draped gracefully over the elbows of the long white gloves hugging her shapely arms. She threw her head back and looked to the stars and turned in a dreamy circle. "This night is incredible!" she yelled to the sky.

"Stefani, I don't know what to say. I should have warned you about going tonight. Travers and I have dealt with each other in the past and—"

"Shhh!" She put her gloved forefinger to her full, soft lips and shook her head. "I don't want to know. I want to be blissfully ignorant. I want to believe that it's no accident we're on this empty pier alone tonight, under the stars without a bunch of business people yakking at me about stock numbers and projections. Without anyone to interrupt our time together. . . Not my mother, not Mr. Travers, not Rachel or anyone else, just you and me. I want to believe that God put us together so we could have a romantic evening away from our house, away from my work, and away from everything that interferes with the way I feel about you."

"Stefani, don't you even want to know why we're here?"

"No, no, I don't. . .I want you to kiss me. I want to finish this night as I imagined it would be. With the man I—with the man I care for."

"Oh, Stefani, I love you, but I have to tell you."

"Shhh!" She came toward him and snuggled into his chest, laying her head on his collarbone. "Tell me you love me again. I don't care about the rest. Not tonight."

"I love you, Stefani."

"John, you are so wonderful. Whoever you are. Whatever you do."

He looked into her eyes and they sparkled with joy. How could he tell her? How could he ruin her faith in him? And yet he knew he must. If he had any decency at all, he had to tell her why she was being punished for his past.

"I know I made fun of you for being blue-collar when we met. I hope you're not embarrassed to tell me what you do.

Because it doesn't matter. . .and anything I said to the contrary was just from a spoiled woman who didn't get her way. I don't care if you dig ditches for a living."

He stepped back toward her. "Actually, Stefani, I do dig ditches for a living. But I do a lot more than that."

"Did you not finish a job for Travers? He's very detail-oriented."

"Uh, no, I finished the job on Travers. That's why he dislikes me so much. I'm an—"

"No!" She pulled away and held up her palms. "Don't tell me. Kiss me."

"Stefani, I—" Before he knew what happened, Stefani's soft lips were on his own. He melted into the kiss, completely forgetting the topic at hand. He pulled her shivering body closer to him and kissed her as he'd never kissed another woman. "I love you, Stefani." Then, he held her shoulders and looked into her eyes. "Your job is in jeopardy."

"Because of you?" she asked quietly.

"Well, because of what I do."

"So what you're trying to tell me is that both my job and my house may soon belong to you?"

"Maybe, but my heart only belongs to you, Stefani. And that's all that really matters."

"Tomorrow is Sunday. A day of forgiveness and worship. I want to worship God without any malice or misunderstanding in my heart. Do me a favor. Tell me Monday. On Monday you can tell me what it is you do and, hopefully, I'll understand. But I need to pray beforehand. I need to go to God, so if you don't mind, just let me enjoy this night under the stars. I'm dressed like a princess and I'm in one of the most beautiful cities in the world with a handsome rodeo star; let me drink it all in."

"You're sure?"

"Kiss me, cowboy."

"You got it, princess."

eleven

Sunday morning Stefani's reality hit her like a wave from the choppy bay. Her mother was seriously ill, her job was in peril, and it looked like she would never meet her goal of owning the duplex. Nothing seemed to bother her as much as her mother's cancer. Guilt plagued Stefani for the lack of love she'd showed Gladys during the recent visit and well before. Stefani prayed and beseeched the Lord for His hand upon her mother, but to everyone else, including John, she remained silent on the subject. She didn't want anyone to judge her for past sins.

Gladys Lencioni was a hard, bitter woman and the cancer had done nothing to change that. The only thing that had changed for Stefani's mother was her fighting spirit. And that scared Stefani more than the cancer. Stefani couldn't remember when her mother approached anything without a battle. Now that Gladys finally had a worthy opponent, she had just given up. Guilt raged through Stefani. If only she'd been a better Christian, if only she'd stayed in Sacramento, if only she'd kept her family name, maybe her mother wouldn't be sick. She knew it wasn't the truth, but it plagued her nonetheless.

Stefani felt wiped out after her prayers and momentarily thought of calling in sick to work. She reasoned her process of combining all the data centers into one central location wouldn't wait, so she scrambled to finish dressing. She trudged to work, hoping to put her problems away and replace them with work's minor inconveniences—knowing that Bob Travers was not going to be happy to see her.

Amy met her at the doorway of her office. "Hi. Bet you never thought you'd see me at work earlier than you."

"I had a rough morning. What brings you in with the

chickens?" Stefani asked, flopping her briefcase on her desk.

"I wanted to hear all the details of the big party cruise on Saturday night. Since I, ahem, wasn't invited, I knew you could tell me who danced on the tabletops and who said something out of line to a shareholder." Amy waggled her eyebrows. "You know, the good stuff."

"Amy, you ought to know me better than that. If there was anything to gossip about, I wouldn't have noticed it or repeated it. I had one purpose for that evening: to mingle with some key investors and, oh yeah, a luxurious evening with a gorgeous cowboy." Stefani clicked her tongue. "*That* was icing on the cake."

"Ooh, this sounds good. Much better than who got drunk," Amy said. "Tell me all about it. What did he wear? Was he a good dancer? Did he kiss you? I told you you'd fall for him."

"Let's just say, I think I could get used to being around John Savitch more often. He's a true gentleman." She thought about mentioning getting kicked off the boat in the middle of the cruise, but she figured that news would get around quickly enough without her mentioning it.

"It's the legs," Amy shrugged. "I knew you wouldn't be able to resist them for long. I told you there was something about a cowboy."

"Amy, he's not a piece of meat for consumption, he's a gentleman. . .that just happens to be a former bull-riding champion," she boasted. "Did you ever think you'd see me with someone that once rode bucking bulls for a living? Do you know he actually charmed my mother?"

"That's actually kind of frightening. If your mom didn't chew John up and spit him out, I'd worry if he was real or not."

"Amy, please don't say that," Stefani closed her eyes, painfully recalling all the harsh things she had said about her mother over the years. Of course, whenever Gladys came to town she proved them with a vengeance, but still Stefani was racked with emotion. Amy knew exactly how Stefani felt about her mother. It was no secret; Stefani had miserably failed in the "honoring her mother" department.

"I'm sorry, Stef. But when did you get so sensitive about your mother? I can't recall anything nice coming out of your mouth about her."

"*Thou shalt honor thy father and thy mother.* I guess I never took that verse to heart before. My mother is getting on in years, Amy. I guess that makes me a little more aware of trying to look past her ways. She's not a Christian, so why should I expect her to act like one?"

"That's true. I never thought about it like that." Amy looked decidedly uncomfortable. She grappled with Stefani's scarf. "Stefani, don't walk around with this guilt. I've heard your mother say some pretty awful things to you over the years. Tell her the gospel, but don't be filled with shame over it. Simply treat her with the respect she deserves as your mother. Okay?"

Stefani grabbed Amy and pulled her all the way into her private office where she shut the door behind them. "She has cancer, Amy. Ovarian cancer." Amy gasped. "Her doctor wants her to have a surgery to determine the extent of it, then possibly follow up with chemo. She was having all these stomach problems. She thought maybe she had an ulcer or something, but apparently not." Stefani began to cry for the first time. She loved her mother. Stefani had been so busy battling for her freedom from Gladys that she'd never taken the time to appreciate all her mother had done right.

"When's the operation? I can cover things here for you; you need to go be with her." Amy held her at the shoulders, beseeching her for a commitment.

"She's not having the operation. She says they're not going to piece her apart and if God's really up there, He can take her whole." Stefani's tears began to flow freely, her shoulders vibrating with sobs. Amy came to her and swept her up in a hug. Stefani just kept crying, using her silk scarf as a handkerchief. "Amy, what do I do? She won't listen to me. She has *never* listened to me."

Amy helped wipe her tears away with a tissue. "This is going to sound kind of rote, but I guess you have to trust God on this one."

"Why can't God let me know what to say or how to act? If I go home and try to take care of her, she'll know something's up. She'll know I think she's going to die because I've never wanted to go back since I left for college. Being in that house with my mother screaming and my dad lounging. . .doing nothing while that ramshackle house falls apart around them. I can't take it, Amy."

"God doesn't want *you* to handle it; He wants to handle it. Stefani, remember when you didn't get the duplex?"

"Of course, how could I forget it? You threw me that stupid party and I had to tell everyone I failed publicly," Stefani laughed through her tears. "Thanks a lot, by the way."

"Hey, what are friends for?" Amy laughed with her. "But do you remember how you thought that it was the end of the world?"

"Yes," Stefani sniffled. "It was."

"Well, life went on, didn't it? And it sounds like you're getting to know your landlord pretty well. I would say God made you a fine trade," Amy encouraged.

"No, Amy, I failed. And worst of all, I failed my grandmother. After I promised her. I don't want to let down my mom, too."

"How can you let down someone that isn't even alive anymore? Stefani, I've never understood your fascination with that land. I can't imagine how any plot of ground could be so important."

"That land belonged to my mom's parents. My grandparents. And before that it belonged to their parents. Nana and Papa begged Mom not to marry my dad. They told her he was just a lazy slouch, that he'd never amount to anything. But my dad was handsome and the pride of the farmlands. He had an athlete's body and a smile that could light up the neighborhood. My mother couldn't help herself."

"So your mom married the man she loved," Amy said dreamily.

"And look what happened. My dad was never the worker my grandfather was. My dad lost the farm for them, the only home they'd ever known. Just like Grandma predicted. I told my grandmother that I would never let that happen to me. That I would own that land again, by myself, and I wouldn't let any man sidetrack me from success."

"And now that your mother's life is in jeopardy, does any of that matter? Your parents have a fine house in Sacramento. Success is not merely financial. Haven't you learned anything since becoming a Christian?"

"Yes, I've learned let your 'yes' be yes and your 'no' be no. I made my grandmother an oath."

"The Bible says not to make any oaths."

"Well, I did make an oath and I intend to keep it. My mother's illness only means my time is running out. I promised to get that land back. And I'm going to do it *before* anything happens to my mother," Stefani said with conviction.

Amy had a look of horror on her face. "No, Stefani. No one cares about that land but you! It's a stupid goal and your grandmother's dead. God said NO!" she shouted the last word.

"No, God said 'not yet.' I want that land to belong to my mother again. So she'll know God loves her. If she sees God gives us the desires of our heart, maybe she'll believe. I'm going to ask John. Not for the whole house, just my side of it."

"Only God can change your mother's heart. You would hurt your relationship with John to keep a promise to someone who isn't even here to see it?"

"I'm not going to hurt my relationship with John. I'm just going to ask him to sell me the house—at least my half of it. If he loves me like he says he does, he'll do it." Stefani said simply. *It's such a basic, natural plan.*

"Why don't you just marry him if you want the house so badly? That would be a nice perk and you'd have the whole house and a nice-looking husband, too."

"I can't marry him for it. I promised my grandmother I'd do it on my own. Besides, he hasn't asked me and I wouldn't say yes for a house. What kind of woman do you take me for?"

"One whose pride and goals have superseded her thought process. John Savitch cares about you, Stefani Willems. Do not destroy what you two have for some inane promise you made your grandmother. You are not responsible for that goal."

"I thought you were trying to make me feel better," Stefani chastised, as she wiped her cheek with the back of her hand.

"I'm trying to show you that your ways don't always work. God's ways do. If you go about this in your own way, you're going to lose John *and* the house."

"Stop preaching at me," Stefani lashed.

A light rapping on the door interrupted their conversation. Amy opened the door a small crack and then opened it wider. John stood in the doorway, then rushed to Stefani when he saw her condition. "Stefani, what's the matter? Did Mr. Travers say something to you?" he asked.

"No, it's nothing like that. What are you doing here?" she asked suspiciously. Stefani was overcome by his appearance. She tried to wipe away any remnants of her tears.

John's voice was low and serious. "We never had that conversation about my job and I think it's important that you know what I do before it's too late." John crossed his brawny arms in front of his muscular chest. His navy T-shirt, worn tan boots, and faded jeans told her she probably wasn't going to like what he did for a living. *Just like my father*, she thought. *Remember what Nana said; don't let your emotions get the best of you. No matter how good he looks. Remember it. Oh, but how I love him.*

Amy stepped between them. "John, this probably isn't the best time. Stefani has had some really tough news."

"About your job?" John inquired.

"No, nothing like that."

"Stefani's mom has cancer," Amy blurted and Stefani threw her an angry stare. He'd seen how she treated her mother. She didn't want him to think she was without compassion. If only she'd known earlier during her mother's visit. Looking at his deep green eyes, Stefani felt the butterflies rise in her stomach. No man was capable of making her feel the way that John did. Her grandmother had to know, she had to understand the power of attraction. That's why Nana warned her so vigilantly. But did Nana understand the power of love? Stefani *loved* John. Did that change anything? Or was it just her mother's weakness repeating itself in the next generation?

"Amy, would you excuse us please?" John held out his arm for Amy to leave. Stefani nodded to her friend and Amy left the office. John shut the door behind her. He sat her in her contoured desk chair behind the great mahogany desk. "How long have you known about your mother?"

Stefani was too weak to lie. "Since that day on the Golden Gate Bridge. She told me when you went to get the car." Stefani wiped her eyes again on her white scarf, which was now covered in black mascara. She tossed it carelessly onto her desk.

"And, what's her prognosis?" John asked.

"She doesn't know. But the doctor did say she needed surgery and possibly a chemotherapy follow-up. None of that matters because she won't do any of it. She hates doctors and thinks garlic is the cure for everything," Stefani said bitterly.

"Stefani, we're going to convince her to get treatment."

"We? John, this isn't your problem. I appreciate your concern, but I'll handle it."

"Just like you handled the house?"

Stefani felt stung. A fresh reminder of her failure—that he'd won. *Well, you won the battle, but I plan to win the war.* "Just please leave. I said I can handle this and I can. Just like I can handle my *own* house. I didn't need your rescue then and I don't need it now. This is none of your business."

"You know I didn't mean it like that. This *is* my business. I love you and I'm not going to let the woman I love go through this trial without being at her side. So clear your weekend; we're going up to Sacramento to talk with your mother," he said flatly. "Why are you being so stubborn? Wasn't it just two nights ago that we ate in a run-down diner with you dressed as the belle of the ball? Did I imagine that?"

She felt hurt momentarily, then regained that stubborn pride and squared her shoulders. "That has nothing to do with this. You're not going to Sacramento with me."

"I am."

"And what if I say no?" Stefani threw her hands to her hips. She'd gotten along fine up until now; she wasn't going to start relying on a man now. Her mother needed her and Stefani would rise to the occasion, just like she always did. He didn't respond right away and she pressed him, challenging him. "And—if I say no?"

"Then you'd better find another place to live, Stefani." He opened the door to leave. "I'm not playing games with you, Stefani. Accepting help may not be your strong suit, but it's time you got used to it. Sharing isn't about life on just your terms. Understand?"

She couldn't say any more. She couldn't believe a man who had treated her so gently and kissed her so warmly could possibly be so brash. He clearly wanted to be in control of her and Stefani would fight him for all she was worth. She'd prove to him that she didn't need him or anybody else.

John looked back at her, but she just turned her eyes away, too angry to let him see how much his threat bothered her. *I'll find a new place to live all right. Right after I get back from Sacramento. Alone. And one day, I will own that duplex.* She'd been sidetracked by John Savitch long enough.

John strode purposely from her office.

Amy walked to the doorway shaking her hand. "Szzzzz. What's got him so hot under the collar?"

"Just when you think you have found a man that's different from all the rest, the *real* man rears his ugly head and tries to take over. They all just want to control you, take over your whole life, so you'll be indebted to them and reliant on them, like some weak little Cinderella. I told you I was better off single, Amy! Why didn't I just leave it at that?" Stefani slammed the door to her office and paced the length of her desk, while she mumbled angrily to herself.

Amy opened the door and peeked in. "Stefani, I may not know John all that well, but he hardly seems the type to want to control you." Amy's face wrinkled in suggestion. "And I hate to remind you, but this isn't the only man you've claimed was trying to control you. All of the others just wanted a commitment from you. Is John any different?"

"Whose side are you on?"

"I'm on your side, Stefani. Which is why I'm telling you that I don't think John is trying to control you, I think he's probably trying to do what's best for you."

"Yes, I know," Stefani said shortly. "That doesn't make him perfect."

"All right, Stef. I'm going to give you the benefit of the doubt. What did he do?"

"He thinks he's going to Sacramento with me to talk to my mom about treatment for her cancer. Can you imagine the mortification on my mother's face if she knew that John knows about her disease?"

Amy stood with her mouth agape, a slow nod forming. "And?"

"What do you mean, 'and'? My mother is sick with cancer, and it's my job to convince her that God cares about her life, that He doesn't want her to perish, especially eternally. Can you give me any reason why John should have any part in that conversation?"

"I can give you three. One, you have absolutely no patience with your mother. John would help keep you calm while you talked to her: a sense of normalcy. Two, John can speak with your father on a level you can't. And three, I think this is too big a battle for you to fight on your own. And *I* can't go with you because I need to make sure this place doesn't fall apart while you're gone."

"But who does he think he is? I haven't asked for his help. He just wants to barrel over me like one of his horses in the rodeo." Stefani crossed her arms violently.

"You haven't asked for help because you never ask for help. You just take everything you can handle and a little bit more, then you become obsessed with it and lock out all the people that care about you. Well, good for John. You won't ask for help, so he's forcing it. Alleluia! It's about time someone got your number."

"He's not going with me," Stefani maintained.

"Then, I think you're going to have a hard time convincing him to sell you half his house," Amy barked.

twelve

"I'm glad you changed your mind about my accompanying you," John said through a smug smile as he drove his SUV down the long, straight rural roadway. *You'd think he was going home.* He had his cowboy hat on, presumably to accompany his standard jeans and thoroughly scuffed boots. Stefani rolled her eyes. *The cowboy has returned.* And so had her animosity toward him.

"I hadn't realized I had changed my mind," Stefani mumbled. "You weren't invited or need I remind you of that?"

"Just think how boring this ride would be with no one to talk to. Nothing but flatlands for miles around." His free hand moved with expression.

"I like it. It gives me time to think," she spouted, hoping he'd get the hint and just leave her alone.

"What are you thinking about?" he asked after a few minutes, his inflection entirely too happy.

"I'm thinking about my mother, John. She's not an easy woman to sway. Once she gets an opinion, she generally sticks with it."

"Who does *that* sound like?" he muttered under his breath.

"I beg your pardon?"

"I said, 'Who does that sound like?' Stefani. The reason you and your mom don't get along is because you are so much alike."

"I am *nothing* like my mother. How dare you say that?"

"Stefani, I know you think my coming along was a bad idea, but I'm going to tell you why I'm here. First of all, you're nicer to her when I'm around. You and your mother have a very destructive pattern of behavior. She nags and you generally run out of the room, say something nasty under your breath, or yell. I'd hardly call that behavior honoring and it certainly won't change your mother's mind. Your mother has lived her entire life with a set of ideals she believes in and you have not respected that. Now, we know she's wrong; she doesn't believe in God's Word and there's no compromising there. But, Stefani, if you would just work with her, showing her respect for what she wants, she might not be so cantankerous. She might see more grace.

"She's lashing out at you because you won't say what she needs to hear. She wants to know you love her and that you appreciate all she did for you, even if it was done with a poor attitude most of the time. Rising above your humanity is what Christianity is all about. You keep falling into your old patterns, because you're not going to God first."

Stefani turned and stared at John. "Is that your version of the five-cent psychologist? My mother knows I love her, John. It's just not something we go around spouting in my house. I've never heard my parents say it."

"I know," he answered sadly. "And that's criminal. I love you, Stefani."

Stefani remained silent, unable to get the words out. She wanted them to come, but they wouldn't; she held them tight in the pit of her stomach. She was too angry, too lost in her own struggle for independence. He wanted to crush her and she wouldn't let it happen. She held tightly to her grandmother's warning: Never let a man get in the way of what you really want. And she really wanted that house. To fulfill her goal.

They drove up to her parents' small ranchette on an acre of dry flatland. Her father hadn't bothered to landscape or plant any crops, so the house carried an abandoned look to it. Retirement took on an added meaning with her father and it suited him. By the looks of the worn paint and dead lawn, it seemed to suit him *too* well. "This is it. Home sweet home. Sheesh, it looks like The Addams Family lives here."

They both laughed before John inserted the voice of reason. "Stefani, that's enough. We're here to edify, remember?" John tried painfully to keep a straight face, but he burst into another hearty laugh.

Stefani opened the screen door and the top hinge fell loose, leaving the door to dangle in an odd, diagonal position. They both erupted into laughter again. Stefani's mother came to the door wearing an old tan floral apron. "What's so funny?" Gladys snapped.

"Mom, the screen door is falling off the hinges. This place looks like something out of an old horror movie."

"Well, tell your father. What he's got to read three newspapers a day for, I'll never know. This house could fall down around him for all he cares. What are you doing here, anyway?"

John intervened. "I've got my tools with me. Why don't I let you get settled, Stefani, and I'll fix the door."

Stefani grabbed his arm. "Don't leave me alone yet," she whispered through gritted teeth.

"You didn't even want me to come, Stefani. Remember?"

"Before you fix the door, come meet my father." Stefani was glad John was so strong: She was going to need him to lean on this weekend. Whether she wanted to admit it or not, she was thankful he'd insisted on coming. The sight of her parents reminded her how difficult the weekend was going to be. She still wouldn't allow John to control her, but she would be happy to lean on him for the weekend.

"Of course, I can't wait to meet your father." John's roguish jawline broke into a warm smile and Stefani took his hand into her shivering one.

"Dad?" she asked, while she picked up pieces of newspaper strewn across the couch and onto the floor. "Dad?" she said a little louder, trying to be heard over the blaring television set. "DAD!" she yelled at the top of her lungs.

Finally, her father looked up slowly. He flicked his glasses down lower on his nose and glared at John's tall frame. Her dad let his eyes roam freely down the length of John, then back up to the steely green eyes Stefani loved so. His gaze came to rest on Stefani. "I thought you didn't like cowboys.

How long you been telling me you wouldn't marry somebody that knew how to work the land? He looks like he knows how to work the land."

"Dad, please!" Stefani pleaded with her eyes, beseeching her father to be quiet. "This is my friend." She felt like she was back at her high school sweetheart dance all over again. Her dad embarrassed that poor boy and scared him off for good. Luckily, John was already familiar with her mother, so he couldn't possibly have imagined her father was much different. "This is John Savitch. He's my landlord. John, this is my father, Bert Lencioni."

"Nice to meet you, Mr. Lencioni." John leaned over and reached out a hand. Bert just nodded in response and picked up his newspaper.

"Aw, call me Bert," he mumbled from behind the paper. "No sense in fancy titles around here. Gladys! Gladys!" he yelled until her mom came back into the room. "Get Stefani and her friend something to eat. Look at her." He peered over the newsprint. "Our daughter's so thin a bird could pick her up and fly off with her. And a big guy like John must need some sustenance after a long drive. Get them some food," he barked as he shifted the paper to straighten it.

"I've got a roast in the oven, but it won't be ready for another hour. Come on, I have a meat loaf left over from last night." Gladys started toward the kitchen and turned around when she realized no one was following her. "Get in here! John! Stefani!" she shouted. Stefani couldn't help but laugh. She hadn't told her parents she was coming and yet, she knew her mother would have enough food to feed an entire house full of guests. No matter how tight the budget was, Stefani's family had always eaten well. For all her faults, Gladys Lencioni took pride in her duties as a wife and mother. Gladys had always thought feeding someone until they were ready to pop was a prime component of mothering.

They followed meekly, with John obviously forcing back his grin. "I love meat loaf, Mrs. Lencioni."

"Stop fawning!" Stefani whispered.

"You've never had my meat loaf. You may think you've had meat loaf, John, but you haven't lived until you try Nana Lencioni's recipe." She sighed deeply. "Nana Lencioni has a nice ring to it, doesn't it, Stefani?"

"Yes, Mother, it does. And I was just thinking about getting a puppy."

Gladys clicked her tongue. "John, what about you, do you want children?"

John shifted uncomfortably in his seat while Stefani grinned like the Cheshire cat. "Uh, I want a wife first," John answered carefully.

"Well, what are you waiting for? You do the asking, so ask!" Gladys stood with her hand on her hip as though John might actually pop the question in her kitchen with her gray eyes boring a hole through him.

Stefani couldn't help it; she burst into a loud laugh. She was beyond being embarrassed by her mother's outlandish comments. "Mother! John's hungry. He's probably saving his proposal until *after* he's been fed," Stefani giggled. "I've heard men never ask women to marry them on an empty stomach."

Gladys took a couple of slices of meat loaf, placed them over two big lumps of mashed potatoes, and smothered them in a rich jelled gravy. When it came out of the microwave, the entire house smelled heavenly. She placed the plate and a tall glass of milk in front of John like he was a child. She stood and waited, hand on her hip, for him to taste the meal. He bowed his head to pray and she tapped her foot impatiently, anxious for her forthcoming compliment.

He shoved a mouthful in and stopped chewing as he savored the flavors. Stefani laughed at the sight of him, relishing the meal with all his expressions. One thing was for sure: She'd come by her culinary talents honestly. Gladys Lencioni could cook.

"I have never tasted anything like this. Stefani, do you have this recipe?"

Gladys intervened. "Of course she does. It's her grandmother's specialty. You can feed an entire house for pennies on that meal. And it sticks to the ribs, too. None of this waking up hungry with this meat loaf." Gladys remained at his side, watching him chew.

"John, do you know how much fat that meal has in it?" Stefani asked. "Of course it tastes good."

"Do you think after tasting this I care?" He winked and Stefani felt her heart react to the stunning sea green eyes gazing at her. Just when she started to think of John Savitch as her best friend, he looked at her that way. A way she couldn't exactly describe but she felt it to her core.

Stefani forced the thoughts of a romantic relationship out of her mind. "Mom, these meals aren't good for you. You need to start eating more fruits and vegetables and sticking to a low-fat diet. I could easily help you pare this down in the calories department and it would still taste good."

"Shhh!" She held up her finger to Stefani and bowed down over her. "Your father doesn't know about the cancer and I don't want him worrying over such things, so you keep your low-fat recipes to yourself. A man works his entire life, he deserves to have a decent meal on the table at night. Low-fat, my eye."

"Mom, what do you mean, 'Dad doesn't know'? How can you keep something like this from him?"

"Your father will only worry. No sense in worrying him over nothing." Gladys went about folding her dish towels into neater rectangles than they already were, nervously looking for something to keep her hands busy.

"Mom, ovarian cancer is not *nothing*. You need to get treatment as soon as possible and you need to tell Dad! If you don't, I will."

"Is that what you came up here for? To pester me? And I don't appreciate you saying that word in front of our guest. Stefani Mary Lucia Lencioni, you will not tell your father anything. The man's got enough on his mind." Gladys pointed her index finger in her daughter's face. "The chicken coop is falling apart, the screen door is off its hinges and the oven door needs to be fixed."

"Mom, the chicken coop is not comparable to your health. And if you don't get help, you could die. Mom, you're not ready to die; you haven't made peace with God and you haven't admitted you're a sinner. And if you think I'm just going to drop this because it makes you uncomfortable, you've got another thing coming! You finally have something to fight, so fight it!"

"Shhh, your father will hear you."

"Mom, I could let off dynamite in here and he wouldn't hear me. He's got the horse races on."

"Stefani!" Gladys sat down and broke into a whisper. "Everybody's got to die of something."

Stefani felt John squeeze her hand under the table. Instantly, she was calmer. "Mom," she said gently, "who is going to take care of Dad if you go? Who's going to cook for him, clean this place? Iron his T-shirts? You can't freeze his meals for the rest of his days."

The fight left Gladys. Clearly, it was something she hadn't thought about before.

"I'm going to fix the door while you ladies talk." John excused himself.

"Mom, Dad doesn't know how to boil water. What do you think would happen to him without you?" Stefani pleaded. Gladys's eyes filled with tears. "I'll tell him if you want me to, Mom. But you've got to fight. For Daddy."

"I don't want to lose this fight," Gladys admitted.

"Then we need to pray, Mom. Because with Jesus in your life, you won't lose. You'll only gain eternal life. But God may have healing in your future; we have to focus on that."

"Does everything have to come back to your religion?"

"I'm sorry, Mom, but for me, it does. Please fight this. For Daddy."

With closed eyes, Gladys nodded affirmatively. "I'll tell

him after you leave and I'll call the doctor on Monday."

After she helped her mother clean up the kitchen, Stefani grabbed a sweater and headed for the front porch. A dingy, lime green lawn chair stood outside the front door just where it had once been at the old clapboard house. The chair was made of heavy-duty rubber cording, but it had weathered many years outdoors and it soothed her to rest in it. She viewed the vast farmlands that surrounded her parents' tiny plot of land. The cornstalks swayed calmly in the breeze and John sat beside her.

"You all right?" John's low voice murmured. His soothing voice was like a cleansing to her heart; she needed his strength and his calmness. She grasped his hand like a lifeboat in a stormy sea.

"Mom's agreed to get the surgery. She'll tell Dad tomorrow."

"It's in God's hands, Stefani. We just need to pray."

"I think I should take a leave of absence from work. Come up here and take care of things for a while. If she wasn't cooking these five-course meals every night, it might make things easier on her."

"Stefani, she lives to make those meals for your father. You can't take her life away; you've got to allow her the freedom to go on as she sees fit. She'll need your help when she's home from the hospital."

"My family. No Ozzie and Harriet here, I'm afraid."

He held her hand, his green eyes wrinkled in a smile. "I'm going to get my tools and fix up the other things around here that need a little attention. Why don't you go spend time with your parents and I'll stay out of the way for a while? I'm enjoying playing handyman. Everything at our house is so new, I feel useless there."

"I'll be sure Mom keeps her plastic milk jugs out of your sight or you'll be growing them a new garden." Stefani laughed.

"Very funny."

"Thanks for being here, John. I really do appreciate it." It took all the humility she could muster. She wouldn't say she loved him, but she could certainly say she appreciated him.

"I'm happy for any excuse to be with the woman I love."

She kicked the dust on the porch with her foot, focusing on the dirt. "I'm still going to talk to Daddy. I think I'm going to tell him about Mom's condition. I'm worried my mother won't do it."

"Stefani, you promised—"

"I never promised, I implied. And I don't think she'll do it without a little prodding. She may have the best intentions, but her follow-through isn't that great. See ya." Stefani planted a friendly kiss on John's cheek and walked back into the house.

Stefani approached her father, and her mother came into the room, wiping her hands on a towel. "Stefani, what are you doing?"

"I'm sorry, Mom, but I have to do this. It's for your own good. Do you want to tell him first?"

"I don't believe you'll do it," Gladys challenged.

"Then you don't know me as well as you think you do, Mom. Dad, Mom has something she needs to tell you." Stefani looked to her mother and if looks could kill, Stefani would be six feet under.

"Bert, I have cancer. Ovarian cancer," she said flatly and headed back into the kitchen. "I've got to get the roast."

Stefani's dad looked up, bewildered. He looked at Stefani for clarification, to see if he'd heard right. "She has what?" he asked.

"She has ovarian cancer, Dad. The doctors want to do exploratory surgery and follow up with chemo."

"Gladys? Get in here," Bert called and Gladys returned from the kitchen, still glaring angrily at Stefani.

"Stefani says you need to get some medical help. That true?" he asked sternly.

"Yes."

"Then you're getting it. Whatever the doctor says."

"Bert, I was going to tell you. I just didn't want to be cut up—"

"And I don't want a dead wife," he interrupted. "When can we schedule this for?" Bert had placed his newspaper down on the brown shaggy carpet. It was the first time Stefani remembered him ever holding a conversation without the paper in front of him. "Is that why you're here, Stefani?"

"Yes, Dad."

"Good for you, honey. You did the right thing."

"Mom, I did a lot of research on the subject and I brought some stuff I thought you'd find helpful." Stefani took the pamphlets and articles out of her briefcase and felt the overwhelming need to run. She didn't want to stay any longer. Her mother and father had serious matters to discuss and Stefani felt very out of place. "I'm going to go."

They made no attempts to talk her out of leaving. Her father simply rose and kissed her forehead. "Thank you, honey. You're a good girl."

Stefani took in a deep breath and grabbed her briefcase. John had fixed the screen door by the time she got to it. "I think we can go now."

"I wanted to fix the chicken coop."

"My parents want to talk. It's awkward in there for me."

"Fine, let me fix it quick and we'll go home. We'll stop and have a nice, leisurely dinner on the way home."

"That'd be nice. John?"

"Yes."

"Thank you."

"You're welcome, Stefani. I'd do it for all the women I love," he said as he winked.

"John, if I asked you another favor, would you do it for me?"

"Of course, Stefani."

"There's no polite way to say this, so I'm just going to blurt it out. Will you sell me the duplex? Not the whole thing, just half of it. My half." Stefani cringed. Was she relying on a man by asking for this favor? Or would this count for doing it herself? She prayed so. She prayed her grandmother would approve. The important thing was that her mother lived to see it. She would own the land her fun-loving father had let slip through his hands.

John studied her for a moment, carefully contemplating the question. "Yes, Stefani. In six months, if you still want to buy it, I'll sell it to you."

"Six months? John, if you're willing to sell it to me, why wait six months? I can pay cash for my half. I've been saving for years."

"You ought to know me well enough to know that I don't care much about money. I have my reasons. Six months and that's my final offer."

"Done," she relented.

thirteen

"Stefani? Mr. Travers wants to see you in his office," Amy announced first thing that Monday morning.

"Now? I've got a million things to do. Is there any way you could reschedule it?"

"He sounds really angry, Stefani. You may want to hustle in there. I think it has something to do with you getting kicked off his yacht that night."

She sighed. *Of all the timing.* "Okay. Will you call Sacramento and see if they got the last mainframe computer up and running? I'm sure Mr. Travers will want a report later today." Gladys's illness had kept their thoughts well occupied and Stefani remembered that she and John had never discussed their cruise again. She had a feeling she was going to wish they had. John's prediction that her job was in jeopardy replayed in her mind.

"Sure thing." Amy saluted as Stefani walked past her.

Mr. Travers luxury office suite was at the top of the five-story building. It took a special elevator code to get the door to open on the suite level. She pressed her number in quickly. Her day planner and a pen with the company logo was all she'd had time to grab from her desk. She hoped he wouldn't quiz her on specific numbers regarding the data center move. With all that occupied her mind, she wasn't prepared for an impromptu report.

Once the doors to the penthouse office opened, Stefani faced a tropical aquarium that served as a barrier wall. Brightly colored yellow and blue fish swam in a luxury-wrapped environment that most *people* only dreamed of. The marble floors led around the aquatic wall and Stefani faced Mr. Travers' secretary, sitting at her threatening black lacquer desk. The older woman held up a finger and finished a phone conversation. Several coworkers sat in the black leather chairs to her left waiting for Mr. Travers' time. No one dared speak. The austerity of the office didn't allow for it. Every sound reverberated off the cold marble flooring.

The phone buzzed and Mr. Travers' secretary spoke quietly into the receiver, then looked at Stefani. "Miss Willems, you may go in now."

Stefani prayed she was prepared for whatever lay in store for her. *Why didn't I press John to tell me more?* Mr. Travers stood as she entered his office, his hands extended toward her. His entire suite was surrounded in windows with a glorious view of the valley. "Sit down, Stefani. I'm just finishing up a call on the speakerphone. Yes, Jim, go ahead."

The voice boomed out of the phone. "So, as far as I see it, the stays have all been tapped out. They've been on this a lot longer than we have, Bob. This guy's not one to mess with."

"I don't want to hear that. Forget the excuses and keep on it." He pressed a button, then turned his attention to her. "We're not closed yet," he mumbled. "Stefani, you've been with us quite a while now." He sat back on the edge of his desk and crossed his arms. He was a handsome man for his age, which she guessed to be near sixty. He was still well built and obviously stayed in shape.

"Yes, sir, I've been with Atlas since college. Ten years now."

"Ten years of good, solid service." He stood and walked back behind his desk. "Which is why I'm prepared to give you such a healthy severance package before you leave." He sat in the burgundy leather chair behind his great black desk.

"Severance package, sir?"

"It seems the Environmental Protection Agency is dogging us again. We're probably shutting down our Silicon Valley site," he said with a shrug. Simply. As though the office was closing early for a holiday. "I'm sure you could tell me a thing or two about the shutdown." His eyes narrowed as though he was waiting for her to relay some kind of information.

"But what about Sacramento, sir? I haven't gotten all the data systems in place there yet. The valley site is pertinent to this business." Stefani sat up on the edge of her seat. She had given her heart and soul to this job. Not to mention that she wasn't fully vested in the last stock options she'd received. Did he honestly expect her to just accept such a statement? "Mr. Travers, you can't fire me. I'm in the process of transferring the data centers to Sacramento," she reminded him. "There isn't anyone else that can finish the process without extensive training."

"Stefani, I'm not firing you."

"Phew." She leaned back again.

"I'm laying you off. There's a big difference. You'll get a severance package and a nice letter of recommendation. If I had wanted to fire you, you'd be gone already."

"Mr. Travers, you can't do this."

"Stefani, I have no choice. If I have to pay the fines the EPA might level against me, I'll be lucky to get out with the shirt on my back. You're one of the highest paid executives on your level. I'm sorry, Stefani, but Ken Donitch can do your job for half the price. And he's willing to go to Sacramento. Are you?"

Stefani thought about living near her parents permanently and the mere idea sent a shiver through her. "I didn't think so. But neither do I think Ken can do the job."

"Well, Stefani, he'll just have to. I don't know what I'm paying these lobbyists in Washington for, but obviously they're not going to see another dime from me until they call off the EPA dogs." He cursed under his breath and Stefani turned away.

"Mr. Travers, I don't understand what the EPA has to do with *my* job. I work in the data center. Nothing I do is even remotely associated with the environment."

"Choices, Stefani. Everyone makes choices in life. Usually, women lead with their heart, which is why men rule the business world."

"Wh–what?" Stefani stammered.

He shoved a stack of papers in front of her. "These are the benefits packages for you to offer your staff."

"My staff?"

"You need to let them go before you leave."

"You want me to fire everyone before I leave?" Stefani was incredulous. If the company was in this kind of trouble, she failed to see how they could offer such generous packages at all. Clearly, something was fishy and it wasn't the lobby aquarium.

"It's all in the contract. The layoffs are part of your severance contract." He shoved another stack of papers in front of her. "A year's salary, plus your latest bonus if you complete your duties here to our satisfaction."

"And my stock options?"

"Fully vested. It's all yours." Stefani watched him in awe. She had always admired Mr. Travers as a self-made man, but there wasn't an ounce of remorse in his eyes. They were dead. Lifeless. Hammered by years of living for greed. No mercy for his employees, only thoughts of himself. Then again, something wasn't quite right; she saw it in his pulsating forehead. She scanned the contract he'd thrust before her. Her eyes rested on the small print. "Said employee waives all rights. . . legal proceedings. . .and any and all future claims shall be settled in binding arbitration with the arbitrator of Atlas's choice."

Bob Travers had never given her anything she hadn't worked heart and soul for. To fully vest her stock options and give her that amount of money could only mean one thing. It wasn't going to be worth anything very soon.

"Mr. Travers, what's this clause about arbitration and lawsuits?"

"Standard legalese. It's to protect ourselves from frivolous lawsuits. You know how greedy people can be."

"Yes, I do." She answered with obvious intention.

"Every company must do it or there wouldn't be a company to protect." He handed her a pen and she met his eyes.

Mr. Travers looked nervous. *Too nervous*, she thought. She didn't break eye contact and noted that for the first time in her career, he broke away from her gaze. Something was corrupt and Stefani was not going to play a part in it.

"I'm sorry, Mr. Travers, but I can't sign this."

"A year's salary, Stefani. You can't afford to walk away from that. You don't have a job, remember?" He let out a laugh, certain she wouldn't turn down the money, but Stefani could see the bead of sweat forming on his brow. "Am I making myself understood? You're unemployed in two weeks."

"I won't fire my staff, Mr. Travers."

"Lay them off, Stefani. Lay them off. There's no guilt in a layoff; it's beyond your control."

"If you want it done, you'll have to do it yourself. I won't do it. I quit."

"Miss Willems, you have spent your entire career with Atlas Semiconductors. You need my letter of recommendation."

"That is blackmail, Mr. Travers, and if I sign that paper, I basically sign away my rights. No deal." Stefani stood to leave and Mr. Travers' demeanor softened.

"Miss Willems. This doesn't need to get ugly. I am offering you a more than fair settlement. You'll need a job and I need you to let this staff go. You're the only one who knows their individual time with the company and how much they're entitled to with the layoff."

"Something isn't right here. I can't put my finger on it, but it doesn't feel right."

The hardened businessman erupted. The truth. Stefani knew she was about to hear it. "This man you brought on my yacht, Stefani." He opened a manila folder on his desk and held up a fuzzy picture of John. John in the soil with a glass vial.

"Yes," she admitted. "He was my date. He's also my landlord," she answered with a shrug. "I fail to see what my personal life has to do with this."

"Stefani, every one of our shareholders saw you with this

man on my boat. This man is a renowned environmental scientist for the EPA. The man is trying to shut this company down. You brought a spy into our midst. You allowed him to collect data and probably shared inside information with him. If you don't sign this agreement, I am free to personally sue you for endangering this company's future profits. And I can't think of a shareholder who wouldn't back me up."

"John is a—" Stefani couldn't finish the sentence. The man she loved, the man who held her house in his hands. The man who said he'd sell it to her in six months. *Six months*. The truth hit her painfully. John *knew* she was losing her job. He knew she wouldn't be able to buy the house. Stefani rose. "You'll have to excuse me, Mr. Travers."

"Stefani, you've got three days to sign this agreement or you'll be hearing from my lawyers."

Stefani scrambled for the door, leaving the paperwork where it lay. She had to get to John. She had to find out his version of the truth. There had to be a misunderstanding. John wasn't an environmental scientist, he was a. . .what? She didn't know. She was in love with a man whose occupation was a mystery to her. *How had this happened? How could I have been so trusting, so stupid?* Her grandmother warned her about men throughout her entire childhood.

"Leave your keys with my secretary," Travers called after her.

Stefani took the elevator to her floor and found Amy. Stefani grabbed her secretary by the arms. "Amy, Amy! What was John doing that day you saw him here? Tell me again."

"He was fiddling in the dirt," Amy shrugged.

"Amy, did he have anything with him? Tools? Wood? Anything?"

"I didn't see anything, Stefani."

Just then two burly security guards got off the elevator. "I'm sorry, Miss Willems, we've been asked to escort you off the property," one of them said.

"But I need to get my things from the office."

"You may take only your handbag and personal keys. Your

personal items including your briefcase will be returned to you shortly along with your last paycheck unless you reconsider Mr. Travers' offer."

Stefani was breathless, but she allowed the men to take her arm. They escorted her to her desk and searched her purse before handing it to her. Then one of them removed Atlas's keys from her key ring. Amy stood, dumbfounded but calm, as they pulled Stefani back into the elevator.

Amy gave her a thumbs-up sign and Stefani watched as the elevator doors closed between them.

❧

John sat at his kitchen table, analyzing lab data on the samples he'd taken the day before. He looked out the kitchen window and saw Stefani drive into the driveway at half past two. *This is it.* The moment he'd been dreading. And the moment he'd deserved for keeping his occupation a secret. He tossed his lab reports aside and dashed over to her house, hoping she was just coming home for a jog. John had told her that jogging alongside work wasn't a good idea. She had heeded his warnings. Of course, John's reasons were environmental, but Stefani had thought they were regarding strangers. Regardless, she had listened and he hadn't pressed it.

Her top button was undone and her shirt untucked from her tailored skirt. "Stefani, your job?"

"You know very well it's my job, John Savitch. How dare you take me to my office party when you knew. . .how dare you use me! All that help for my parents, fixing their chicken coop, charming my mother, it was all a lie!" Her lips began to tremble and soon a single tear fell from her eye. "Did you think I'd thank you for saving me from buying this house? Because you knew I was about to lose my job?"

"I thought I was protecting you from toxic chemicals." It was a stretch trying to make half of the truth seem to be enough. He prayed for strength to set the record straight. "No, Stefani, that's not all of it. I wanted you to fall in love with *me*—as a cowboy, not an environmental scientist. You seemed so convinced you couldn't fall for a workingman. I wanted to show you I was worthy of you as a cowboy. Then, I just got farther and farther into my research and then I realized it was too dangerous to tell you. I didn't want you held responsible and I couldn't risk having you confront Travers before my report was finished. It was a mixture of consideration, professional responsibility, and cowardliness."

"With an emphasis on cowardliness. How dare you make that choice for me!"

"Did I make that choice? You seemed to be pretty content being in the dark about my occupation. You never insisted on knowing what I did; in fact, you didn't want to know. You didn't want to admit you were going out with a working-class man, so you never asked!"

Her expression acknowledged the truth in his statement.

"You're not going to blame this on me, John Savitch. My grandmother warned me never to get involved with a handsome man. I did just what she said I would; I justified your behavior because I wanted you. And now, my chances of meeting my goal are null and void. I have no job, no home. . . nothing all because of you."

"You have a home. You'll always have a home. That house is yours. With rent or without, Stefani."

"You must be kidding. Do you think I'd take anything from you after what you did? You wormed your way into my heart, playing this remarkable Christian man, and all the while you lied to my face."

"Stefani, I may not have acted Christlike, I admit that. But don't question my faith or my love toward you. I sinned, yes. But I did it to protect you. Knowing about a toxic plume has huge consequences for employees. People have been killed for it! Didn't you see that movie *Silkwood*?"

"Such drama! I suppose this is where I rush into your arms and praise you for rescuing me—fall at your feet and sob?"

"Oh, Stefani, no. This is where I beg you for your forgiveness for acting like such a pompous heel and for thinking I knew what was best when I wasn't acting in God's will. The fact is, neither of us have been acting in God's will or we wouldn't be in this mess."

"I have my mother to think about. I can't be worrying about this. . .this nonsense. Consider this my thirty-day notice." Stefani turned on her heel and headed for the house.

"Stefani, please talk to me. We need to talk about this."

"I have nothing more to say to you. You need to concentrate on finding a new renter."

"I love you, Stefani. I know that probably doesn't mean much at this juncture. But I do love you."

"You cowboys have an odd way of showing it."

fourteen

After a restless night, Stefani slept in Tuesday morning. It was so refreshing to sleep until the sun became so bright that it nudged her gently from her state. She opened her Bible and prayed for God's guidance in finding a new job. She actually felt excited at the possibility of a new challenge. She'd been at Atlas her entire career; surely there had to be more to life than this one company. More to life than work that bled you dry and fired you.

But just when she started to feel joy, the memory of John crushed any hope for her future. He was a stranger. A man she never knew. Tears flowed again and the oddest thing happened. Stefani wanted to see John. She wanted to cry on his shoulder and share her pain with the man she loved. *Why? Why didn't I heed my grandmother's advice?* It was too late now. She loved the man.

She rolled out of bed and made herself a cup of strong coffee. She breathed the rich scent deeply and ran out to the driveway to get her newspaper. The sooner she got to the want ads and started distributing her resume to headhunters and former colleagues, the better. She would devote herself to her job hunt and her mother. She wouldn't have time to think about him. John's newspaper was still in the driveway as well, and Stefani sprinted back inside before she would chance seeing him.

She sat at the kitchen table with her coffee and unfolded the paper in shock. There on the front page was John's picture. She read the photo caption: "John Savitch, Leading EPA Scientist, Does It Again." The headline above it, in big black letters: "ATLAS SEMICONDUCTORS SHUT DOWN, EPA CALLS IT A POISON MILL." And in smaller letters: "Workers turned away."

Stefani's breath left her and she read the headline again and again, then lowered her eyes to the story:

John Savitch, a leading environmental scientist for the Environmental Protection Agency, has won a first for the people of Silicon Valley after a string of successful closings in his home state of Colorado. After following up a lead from unnamed sources, Savitch and his partner, Tom Cook, discovered a toxic plume six thousand feet wide and five hundred feet deep under the manufacturing plant of Atlas Semiconductors. Savitch is quoted as saying, "Travers actually told his employees he was going to put a workout, fitness station on top of the very spot that recorded some of our highest readings."

Stefani tossed her newspaper down. *How could he?* He had actually quoted her verbatim, and never even told her what he did for a living. He had worked his way into her heart, all the while systematically shutting her out of a home and a job, and even possibly destroying her career reputation. Stefani paced her kitchen, panting with her anger. She mumbled to herself, letting out a stream of harsh words, hoping he might just overhear her. She should have let her staff go. It would have been easier coming from her. Travers must have thought they had more time. The EPA had obviously acted before Travers could.

Her heart dropped. She'd give anything to just make this all go away. She wished it was all a bad dream and she'd wake up. But every time she tried to start the day over, she opened her eyes to that newspaper. John's exasperatingly handsome face staring back at her, mocking her—mocking any semblance of love she had for him.

Why didn't it occur to me that he had a real job? Why was I so blind, so trusting, so. . .naive? She had thought him an uneducated cowboy, straight from the back roads of Colorado, but when she searched her memory she knew she had only herself to blame. He'd been to college; he knew Shakespeare. He could name each of the brightest stars as they appeared in the evening sky upon the ridge. "How could you be so stupid, Stefani?" She whacked herself across the forehead. "How could you have been such a snob and be blinded by that fake cowboy charm?"

He was everything she had wanted in a man, except he was none of it, because it was all what she wanted to hear. He'd made her believe he was something she needed. He must have known the first day when he'd seen her name on her business card. That had to be the reason he called her to rent the duplex. She let her head fall onto the kitchen table with a bang.

The doorbell rang and Stefani picked up the crumpled newspaper and marched to the door, her seething anger rising ever higher to a boiling point. She opened the door hard and instead of a repentant John, it was Amy.

"What does John have to say about this?" She held up the paper.

"Nothing. He did it; he's an environmental scientist." Stefani was truly wounded. Here she was, alone and worse for the experience. "You told me friendship grows people; well, I trusted him. I did what you said and look how far it got me. I'm jobless, boyfriendless, and soon, homeless."

"Stefani, it's a job. Who cares? They weren't paying us what we were worth anyway. This valley is teeming with jobs. It's not like we live in the middle of nowhere. We'll have a job by the end of the week. I'm sure John is just sick over this."

"How can you possibly defend him, Amy?"

"I'm not defending him, I'm just reminding you. It was you that didn't want to know what he did for a living. It was you who was embarrassed by his jeans and lack of education. If he didn't tell you what he did for a living, I can't help but think that was your doing, Stefani."

"I don't know why he kept his work a secret, Amy, but I'm about to find out. Make yourself at home. There's coffee on the counter." Stefani climbed up the stairs and threw on a pair of jeans and a T-shirt. She reached for her boots, then hesitated before grabbing her familiar loafers instead. She brushed a light spattering of powder on her face and climbed back down the stairs. "Will you be here when I get back, Amy?"

"Where am I gonna go?" Amy flopped on the couch and flipped on a talk show. "It's not like I have a job."

"Did you take the severance package?" Stefani asked.

"Of course, everybody did," Amy answered.

"No. I didn't," Stefani admitted.

"Stefani, how do you expect to wait it out until you get a new job? The right job?"

"I'll just have to get one soon. I'll pray," she said simply. "I need to talk to John. I have a feeling he's waiting for me. His paper is gone, so he knows by now."

"You want me to come for moral support?"

"No, I can handle it."

She rang the bell and he answered immediately.

"Good morning, Stefani." He opened the door wider and Stefani avoided his gaze and walked in. She heard the door shut behind her and she suddenly became fully aware of his presence. Aware of his athletic shorts and running T-shirt and even of his bare feet. Whenever Stefani was alone with John she felt that magnetic pull between them, something absolutely invisible that felt like an elephant in the room no one could mention. The attraction between them was lethal and it was the reason he and Stefani usually went to public places like the ranch for their dates. The intimacy of close proximity was embarrassing to them both; to have such a sizzling reaction and fight it without admitting it existed.

She felt it even now. Even when he may have been responsible for ruining her entire structured life. "I see you have today's paper," he continued.

"Congratulations, you're a hero." Stefani tossed the paper on his countertop as she headed for the dilapidated couch in the living room.

John followed her and his tone was biting. "Would you rather I left you to die an early death of cancer from working on top of dangerous levels of trichloroethylene?"

"Don't use your big words on me, cowboy. If you had wanted to impress me with your education, you should have done so a long time ago when I asked what you did for a living. Because right now, I'm not impressed."

"I wanted to prove to you that you were capable of loving someone, no matter what they did. But now, I'm not so sure you are," he added bitterly. She sat on the couch, but stood quickly when she realized she had far too much animosity to just sit still.

"You're going to blame ruining my life on the fact that I'm not emotionally tender? That I'm not a sweet-natured doormat?" she asked incredulously.

"Stefani, I have told you many times what you mean to me, how I love you, and I've never heard a smidgen of the sentiment returned. You've never said how you feel once, not when you kissed me, not when I said I loved you. The only response I ever got was: 'Can I buy my half of the duplex from you?' Was that the proof you needed from me?"

"After you've destroyed my life, you want me to admit I love you?"

"I didn't destroy your life, I may have saved it. Cancer obviously runs in your family, anyway. Working around toxic pollutants couldn't help."

"You leave my mother out of this; she has nothing to do with it."

"She has everything to do with it, Stefani. If you would tell her how much you love her instead of trying to take care of everything, you might break her hard shell. If you'd let God work instead of trying to plan every moment of your future, you might be surprised how He handles things."

John was just fighting dirty. "You're just trying to keep the subject off of *you*. *You*, John Savitch from Colorado, the man who singlehandedly brought down a multimillion dollar corporation. You, who put hundreds of people out of work today and you, who lied to someone you supposedly loved to score some kind of career goal."

"Isn't that what you did to me? You have something to prove about this house. You used my love for you to get me to sell it to you."

"But your goal was more carefully planned, wasn't it, John?"

"You know me better than that. Mr. Travers had the opportunity to do things right when he came to California. He'd already lost one business in Colorado by cutting corners. You didn't know that, did you? This was his chance to make things right, but still he put the profit margin above any concern he had for you or any of his employees. If you think Bob Travers is your friend, you tell me why you didn't sign that little severance agreement he gave you?"

"How did you know I didn't sign that agreement?" Stefani fell to the couch, her astonished eyes wide with inquiry.

"Because his lawyers tried to hire me as Atlas's exclusive environmental consultant, that's how. That's where the newspaper got that quote they used by me today. From Bob Travers' lawyers."

"If you had *told* me what Mr. Travers was allowing to happen, I might have been able to fix things. I could at least have gotten the data center moved to Sacramento and saved more jobs. Why couldn't you trust me with the information you had?"

"It's my job, Stefani. I couldn't—"

Stefani stood. "You couldn't jeopardize *your* job, but my job? No problem. After all, you own the house, not me, so what do *I* need a paycheck for. I'm just a woman, is that it? I can go find some man to take care of me, get married, have a couple kids, and forget all about my high-powered job. Except, that was never going to happen, John. But that was your plan all along, wasn't it? To bring down Stefani Willems and her prideful ways. Well, congratulations, John. You've done it. I bow before your feet. You've won." She bowed an exaggerated curtsy at the waist in royal fashion. "You are smarter, tougher, and more determined than I. I admit it. I bow down before the master."

"Stefani, stop it." John came to her and forced her eyes up to his. They were still so pure, their sea green making her want to dive into their depths. If she allowed herself to look much longer, she'd forget all about her pain, all about his lies. She saw love in those green eyes, concern like she'd never felt before, and she wanted to fall into his wide chest and weep with all that was within her. To rest in his strength. *John, I love you. I love you, I love you. How could you betray me?* She fell against his chest for a moment, breathing in the deep, earthy scent mixed with musk cologne. So familiar and so agonizing all at once. She never wanted to pull away, but it was now or never and she willed herself from his arms.

Her tears came, any hope of hiding them now hopeless. "John, how could you?" she cried, while pulling away from him. "You had ample opportunity to tell me what you did. I was wrong when I said it didn't matter what you did. Because it does matter. I want my simple cowboy back, the blue-collar, considerate man of God I thought you were. I liked the cowboy better than the environmental scientist. A lot better." She reached for the door and shut it quietly behind her. Outside, the rain clouds were forming above with a light sprinkle coming down. She ran for shelter, covering her head. Summer was over and so was the love affair of her lifetime. She would never love again as long as she lived. She was certain of it.

Stefani didn't feel like facing Amy when she returned to her duplex, but Amy was on the edge of her seat, waiting for her return. "Well, I'm dying; what did he say?" She flipped off the television and leaned her elbow on the sofa arm.

"Nothing," Stefani shrugged. "Nothing we didn't already know. I'm going back to bed, Amy. Make yourself at home."

"Stefani."

"I don't want to talk about it. He doesn't have any excuses, Amy. He kept the truth from me, plain and simple, and we pay the price. End of story." Stefani clambered up the stairs and shut her bedroom door with a slam. Her Bible lay before her and she turned away from it. "God, how could You do this to me? You've left me here with nothing! Nothing, God! I've got an ill mother that thinks You're a figment of my imagination. No job and no money because You told me not to sign that agreement. I gave You my heart and this is where You lead me? Father, I love John. I love him with everything that's in me, even though I know it's wrong. He's no different than any of the other men who lied to me and moved on. Those who said they wanted a career-oriented, educated woman, but couldn't handle it in the long run. . . Oh, Lord, I'm desperate. Why did You give me John at all, if he was just going to betray me? Make this all go away. Please. Give me a reason to understand what he did."

"YOU SHALL KNOW THE TRUTH." She kept hearing that verse in her head. Except, she knew the truth, but it had only caused pain, not relief. What was God trying to tell her?

A knock sounded at her bedroom door. Opening it, she started to apologize. "Amy, I—" It was John, standing tall, firm, and confident in a gray business suit. His expression told her he wasn't going to walk away without saying his piece and he leaned on the door frame with fingers laced around its edge. She looked up at the rugged fingers worn from work and play. "You apparently have something to say, so go ahead. Since you've managed to sweet talk your way past Amy, you've gotten your way, but what else is new? My feelings seem to count little in the scheme of things."

"I'm going to ignore that, because I think if you search your heart, you know the truth, Stefani."

"And whose truth would that be?" Her fists went to her hips and she tried to look as determined as he did.

"This," he pointed down at her, "is the Stefani Willems I first met. Snippy, immature, and vengeful. And personally, I don't want any part of *that* Stefani Willems."

The fire left her and she was stunned silent. He thought

she was snippy and vengeful? There was not much she could do with that information. "So what is it you want, John, if it's no part of me?"

"To give you these." She opened her palm and he dropped a set of keys into it.

"What's this?"

"It's a symbol. I will take care of you, if you'd let me. If you'd stop fighting me every step. It's my keys to your house. The place is yours as long as you want it."

"You want me to take charity from you?" Surely, things weren't that desperate.

"No, I want you to accept some help until you get back on your feet and a new job. I don't think you know what you're up against with Bob Travers. He's a spiteful man, Stefani, and he's not likely to let you run free with the information you have on his company." John's jaw was clenched and firm, and his gentleness seemed long gone. He was robotic in form and it crushed her. His words may have offered her his assistance, but his stance told her it was his Christian duty, not from an overwhelming love for her.

But that's what I wanted, wasn't it? I didn't want to be dependent on any man. So how is today any different from yesterday? Because today, she was back to square one with the attractive cowboy from Colorado, right when they'd met. The arrogant, selfish, condescending. . .wonderful man she loved.

"Is that your plan, John? To be my knight in shining armor and come rescue me from my reckless life, the life *you've* turned into a battleground?" Why did her mouth ramble misery, when she willed it to be sweet and pure? Where was this awful division coming from?

His jaw flinched but otherwise she saw no outward sign of anger. "No, Stefani," he said evenly. "I could never rescue you. You'd never allow it, even if you needed my help beyond reason, you'd never humble yourself to take it. This is not charity." He looked down at the keys. "This is my peace offering to leave on a good note. You'll find another job soon and I'm going back to Colorado. I did give you first right of refusal on the house. Did I not? Get a job so you can buy it with that small fortune you've saved up."

Fear enveloped her. John leaving? *Oh, Lord, no.* Why couldn't she just tell him she loved him and that she couldn't imagine life without him? *I love you, John. Why can't I just say it?* Because it wouldn't come.

John continued. "I'm sorry for the pain I caused you, both directly and indirectly. I've repented of my silence many times, but now I offer it to you with my sincere apologies. I would never have hurt you intentionally, Stefani. I'd make it up to you, if you'd only give me the chance." There was no joy in his serious eyes, his laugh lines were almost invisible, and his straight, sculpted jaw offered no sign of falling into his ready smile. "Tell your mom I'll be praying for her." He turned and started down the hallway.

"Wait. When will I see you?"

"I'll be out of town for a few days. I'm looking into buying a new horse."

"Do you want me to take care of Kayla while you're gone?" She thought this was the olive branch necessary, but he snubbed it.

"No. Her trainer's taking care of her. Thanks, though."

"John?" *Say it, Stefani, just say it. Three little words, just say them!* "Good-bye."

Where should she even start to pick up the pieces? With her mother? Her job? What was the priority? What did God want her to do?

fifteen

The duplex was lonely without John. Although Stefani had lived alone for nearly twelve years, fear gripped her at night with his side of the house dark and silent. She hadn't realized how much she'd come to rely on his safety checks and just knowing he was there. Ready to help at any sign of trouble. Of course, they lived in one of the safest neighborhoods available, but being alone now troubled her deeply.

Stefani packed her things and prepared to be at her mother's side when Gladys came out of surgery. Gladys had asked that Stefani not be there beforehand and Stefani had obliged. The long drive to Sacramento was a blur. She arrived at the hospital to find her father in the surgical waiting room. Bert had his three newspapers, but they were folded neatly beside him, his own burdens a priority.

"Stefani! Oh, honey, I'm so glad to see you."

"Hi, Dad. Heard anything yet?"

"No, the surgeon said it would be anywhere from forty-five minutes to four hours. She's been in there about two hours now."

"I've been praying for her, Daddy. God will provide."

"I hope so, honey. Your mama's a fighter, but the information the doctor gave us doesn't offer much hope—if it's bad."

Just then, the doctor came in. He removed his green surgical hat, revealing his bald head. He seemed totally bewildered. "Mr. Lencioni?"

"Yes?" Bert grasped his daughter's hand tightly.

"There's no cancer."

"Did you say no cancer? What about the sonograms? Her symptoms?"

"I can't explain it, Mr. Lencioni. I can only tell you what I know now. There's not a spot of cancer in your wife. She had all the symptoms of advanced ovarian cancer."

Bert sat down and wept with the news, holding his face in his hands. Stefani had never seen such a sight. She sat beside him, unsure of whether or not to intrude upon his overwhelming emotions. Stefani felt triumphant. She knew God had cured her mother. God had given her more time to share His love and awesome healing. It was the only explanation.

"Oh, Stefani, I can't believe it."

"I told you people were praying."

"My beautiful daughter. What a delight you are, spreading such sunshine about. Thank you for being here." He grasped her hand tightly.

"I wouldn't be anywhere else, Dad. I'm here to take care of you and Mom until she's up and around from surgery."

"What about your job?"

"I'm looking for work. Don't you worry, I'll be fine."

Stefani's father held a vigil over Gladys until she awoke. They whispered and giggled to one another and Stefani left to give them their privacy. Their intimacy brought forth so many memories. So many times she dreamed of being loved by a man like her father. Gladys Lencioni was his princess. Bert didn't seem to mind her mother's obvious character flaws. When did that dream end? When did Stefani become so cynical about men?

The following day, Stefani finally got some time alone with her mother. Gladys was weary from the wear on her body and slept throughout the day. But just before dinner, Gladys awoke. "Stefani?" she croaked.

"Yes, Mom, it's me."

"Oh, Stefani, I'm so glad you're here. Did you hear about the cancer?"

"Yes, Mom, I am thrilled."

"That surgeon expected me to be riddled with the stuff, didn't he?"

"I think so, Mom."

"Where's your cowboy?"

"Mom, he's not *my* cowboy."

"Stefani?"

"John and I had a falling-out."

Gladys sat up, grimacing in pain as she moved. "What do you mean?"

"I mean, we're through," Stefani said simply.

"Stefani Lencioni, it'd had better be the drugs I'm hearing."

"No, Mom, it's true. You didn't even like John."

"Who says I didn't like John?"

"You were always telling me that he didn't have a real job and explaining to me he was too good-looking to be useful."

"I always talk about your boyfriends that way."

"So, what's your point, Mom?"

"John's the only one that didn't run. Ain't he?"

"No, Mom, he didn't run, but that's because he was busy. Busy with his *real* work of putting me out of a job. He lied to us, Mom. He's no cowboy; he's a highly educated environmental scientist of all things. He works for the EPA, shutting down polluting businesses."

"He never lied to us, Stefani. All you had to do was look at his crazy work hours and his fancy house to know he had some important job. You just weren't looking."

"Mom," Stefani answered condescendingly, "that house belongs to us. It was our land and he's only been the last obstacle in my way. I'm going to own that land again, Mom. And when I do, you and Daddy are going to come back and live there again."

"Stefani, I don't want to live back there again. And I certainly don't want an elegant house where I can't even work the fancy stove. What is all this about?"

"I know why you sold the land, Mom. Grandma Willems told me. I wouldn't trade Daddy for anything; he's been so loving and kind. But Mom, he was never a hard worker and Grandma told me how his negligence led to the sale of your parents' farm."

"What?" Gladys rubbed her eyes. "What exactly did Grandma tell you?"

"She told me that when you met Daddy, you tossed all caution to the wind and married him against their will. Their only hope for you was to give him the farm. She said the apricot orchards needed hard work, but Daddy was always off doing what he wanted and never had time to care for the trees. So when the taxes increased and came due, you had to sell. But John is going to sell me the land, Mom. I'm going to own it again. I know we won't ever have the orchards again, but we will have the land again."

"Stefani, we don't want that land in our family. Whatever gave you that crazy notion?"

"What do you mean? Mom, God provided it. It's yours again as soon as I get a job; John said he'd sell it to me. You don't have to be brave with me. It's okay to admit Daddy lost it."

"Stefani, have you ever seen your father do something for himself that didn't involve you or me? Other than read the papers and watch television?"

Stefani contemplated before answering. "No."

"If he went fishing or to a ball game, did he ever go without you?"

"No."

"Think about it, Stefani, would your father have ever sold that land without a reason?"

"I don't understand."

"Your grandmother was a wonderful woman, but she had one very black blind spot when it came to your father."

"I promised her I'd get the land back, Mom. Without a man, and I will."

"Stefani, you are not responsible for an unreasonable request made by a senile old woman. Go back home and get your cowboy and forget about this nonsense."

"No, Mom, I promised."

"Do you remember when I told you that story of the neighbor who went to church every day? The one who came home to get beat every day because the preacher kept telling her that divorce was sinful?"

"The reason you hate the church? Of course I remember, Mom. It sickens my soul that you hold God responsible for man's sin."

"That wasn't a neighbor. That was your grandmother, your aunt, and me. Your grandfather used to beat us all with a belt until we were black and blue. Sometimes just because we didn't hang the wash out correctly. My father was a hard drinker and a hard worker. His expectations for your father were ridiculous. Of course, Bert could never measure up. No one could have. But when your father came along, the beatings stopped immediately. Your father would have killed your grandfather if he'd laid a hand on us again. Sure, your papa wasn't the hardest worker, but that was his choice."

"But Grandma said—"

"Grandma said a lot of things, Stefani. Especially when she got older. I think she started to blur Bert with your grandfather. In the end, she just equated all men with the evil Grandfather inflicted on her. It broke my heart to see you living on that property again," Gladys admitted. "I thought that land was cursed. But now I see it brought you John, so I guess there is gold at the end of the rainbow."

"Grandma told me Daddy lost the farm because he was lazy."

"No, honey, Daddy sold the land to pay for your college expenses. We moved up here where it's cheaper so that you could afford Stanford's expenses."

"You bought that ramshackle house. . .so I could get an education?"

"We like that house, Stefani. Your father's getting on in years and keeping it up is just a bit much for him. If there's one thing I learned in this lifetime, it's that stuff don't matter none next to people. You were our priority, Stefani. Always have been. You were so smart. You deserved to go to Stanford. But we didn't sacrifice nothing, Stefani. That land was full of pain for me. If it weren't for your father, I could never have lived there as long as we did. Your father taught me to be content where I was."

Stefani forgot to breathe. "I've been working for nothing all these years. Everything I thought was true was just a lie. I wanted you to believe in God again, Mom. I thought if you knew that God took care of your needs—"

"Stefani, it's too late for me and God. I stopped needing Him a long time ago, when your father came along."

"No, Mom. Read the Bible again. You still have so much healing to do."

"If it makes you feel better, I'll read it, honey. Now you go home and make Papa some dinner. He'll be getting hungry soon."

"But, Mom—"

Gladys was swept away by sleep. Her tired lids fluttered closed.

❧

Stefani stepped onto her parents' porch two days later and found the screen door in fine working order. John's gorgeous smile filled her heart. His legacy was everywhere around her parents' home. She missed him terribly. Her goals for the house were long gone—replaced by the real desire to have a man who loved her like Bert loved Gladys. *Who would have ever thought I would have desired something my mother held?*

Her mother's screeching voice met her at the porch. "What? You don't have to work?" The older woman appeared in the doorway. "Screen door works great and you should see the chicken coop. That's some handyman you got there."

"Hi, Mom." Stefani came toward her mother and wrapped her arms around the wide frame. "How are you feeling?" She took Gladys' free arm and helped her father get Gladys inside.

"Like somebody shot me full of holes. How should I feel?"

"Come on, Mom, let's get you into bed."

"What's wrong with you?"

"Mom, nothing's wrong."

"My daughter, who never takes a day off in her life, sits at the hospital, cooks for her father, then stays in the middle of a weekday to wait on me? Something's wrong. I thought I told you to go home and get that cowboy. It ain't every man that can fix a chicken coop."

"Come on, Mom, let's get you into bed. It seems your fighting spirit has returned."

"Don't get smart with me, young lady."

"Hi, Dad."

"Hi, honey. Did you get your mom's bed ready?" her dad asked.

"I sure did. She's all set. I moved the TV in there and everything."

"I can't be sitting around watching television." Gladys allowed Bert to help her into bed. "Bert, you roll that TV back out there and go watch the races. You're making me nervous hovering over me. Stefani and I will be fine." Bert smiled and did as he was told.

"Are you feeling any better?" Stefani asked, while she pulled up the covers over her mother.

"I feel tired," her mom admitted. Her mother was sweating from the taxing walk.

"Do you want something to eat?"

"Nothing you'd make. None of your fat-free, tasteless meals you make for health. Who wants to live if I get to eat cardboard for dinner?"

Stefani ignored the comment. "I'm glad you had the surgery. Don't you feel better knowing you're healed?"

"Your friend said I'd feel better knowing. Also said he'd be praying. He's a smart boy, I trust him." Gladys nodded.

"My friend?" Stefani inquired, her brow furrowed with confusion.

"John. He was here to fix the barn door last week. I fed him good while he was here, don't you worry. And he got enough fat to keep him going through the day."

"John was here? You mean when I brought him. . .right?" *Did her mother possibly say what she thought she said?*

Gladys picked at the bedspread. "No, he was here again before my surgery. He came by to fix that gate that's been opening on its own and letting the goats wander. He was on his way somewhere, said something about buying another one of them big dogs of his."

"You mean a horse?"

"I suppose. Your father just pointed him in the right direction. Nice boy. Anyway, he told me about his mom. Such a shame. You know he lost his mom when he was only ten to breast cancer?"

"He told you that?" Stefani actually felt hurt that John had shared his most intimate secret with her mother, but not with her. *Why had he come here? What could have been his motive? Did he just want to make sure my mom didn't suffer the same fate or was it something more? Is he the considerate, loving caretaker or the reckless liar who played with my future?* What did it matter? He was leaving California and Stefani, as well.

"Now, Stefani, you have a life of your own to lead. Your father won't have you sitting around, waiting on us." Gladys pulled her hand away.

"Mom, I don't have a job to go to, so don't worry. Just concentrate on getting better."

"And I'm supposed to worry about you instead? No, Stefani, you go home and get a new job."

"Mom, I need some time to think. All the information you gave me this week is just so overwhelming. I'm not ready to work yet. I was focusing my entire career on getting that land. Now what do I have to work toward? Suddenly, my life seems so meaningless. I wish God would just tell me what to do."

Her mother broke her vocal ranting with her old-fashioned common sense. "You're not staying here, Stefani. You've got your own life back in the Bay Area. You're not going to give up your life to take care of us. We've got a good health plan and I've frozen enough dinners to last your father a month. I want you to go back home. We'll get you some money, but John said he'd take care of the rent for a while."

"Mom, I want to stay and I don't need any money."

"You're young and you've got your entire life waiting for you. I won't have you put it on hold to play nursemaid. Besides, you're not exactly the nursing kind; that's why we sent you to business school."

"Mom, I *want* to be here."

"All the same, I want you to leave. You can pray for me if it makes you feel better. John says you've got a home as long as he's in California, so go back and get him, Stefani. I don't know what happened between you two, but it'll do no good to have you here and him there. Now go home and get married."

"John doesn't want to marry me, Mom, and he certainly never asked me. John was only using me to get information on my company to bring down the mighty Bob Travers."

"If you believe that, that Stanford education didn't do a thing for you. Go home, Stefani." Gladys pointed a stern finger at her daughter.

"John's not even home. He went back to Colorado and I don't know when, or even if, he'll be back."

"He'll be back. You just get there first and make him his favorite dinner when he comes home. I don't know what you think he did to you. But men don't drive two hours out of their way to fix barn gates for people they hardly know. He loves you. Even your uneducated mama can see that."

"He loves God and he was probably doing his Christian duty by fixing up around here."

"Go get him, Stefani. Do you think your father just came and asked me to marry him? I had to be available and know when to play hard-to-get. Well, you've played your games; now it's time to come clean and collect your husband."

"I'm not playing games. I'm a Christian woman and the man that God chooses for me must become mine without any games. Games are dishonest." Stefani squared her shoulders.

"Well, fine, but I know a man sometimes needs a little push in the marriage department and you're not getting any younger. It's time you stopped relying on that God business and started getting busy. Otherwise, I'll never have a grandchild. I don't understand it, Stefani. You're a fine-looking woman, so what is it you say to men that makes them run away?"

"Mom, have you heard a word I've said? Have you bothered to listen to anything I've come here to say today? I'm not getting married!" Stefani was ready to attack her mother further when she heard that tiny voice within her, not even a whisper, yet loud and clear.

YOU SHALL KNOW THE TRUTH.

What is the truth, Lord? I asked for prayer for my mother, for her healing, for her salvation, and she's still the same hard woman, Lord. You may have healed her cancer, but her heart is as hard as ever.

Stefani found her favorite lawn chair on the porch and opened her Bible. Philippians 2:3 was highlighted on the open page: "Do nothing out of selfish ambition or vain conceit, but in humility consider others better than yourselves." Stefani's sin hit her with the weight of a freight train. Everything she had worked for had been for her own glory, not for God's. She wanted the land to prove to her mother that God was real, but all it really proved was that Stefani had been so set on her own agenda, she'd never heard what God wanted.

John was right. Stefani *was* just like her mother: stubborn, strong-willed, and trying to be worthy. Worthy of acceptance by others, instead of God. She fell to her knees, begging God for forgiveness. *Lord in heaven, I have tried so hard. So hard to be who I thought You wanted me to be. But now I realize I was being what I thought people wanted me to be: successful, rich, independent. I tried it all on my own power. And here I sit, unemployed and lonely. You never cared about that house, but You used it to give me my true heart's desire: a man who loved me like my father loved my mother. Why didn't I hear You knocking? Why couldn't I see what You were trying to say to me? Oh, Lord, I have been so selfish, so vain, and so full of myself. Without You, I can do nothing. I admit that to You now and beg You to help me. I want to be on the right track. I want to do Your will. No matter what that is, Lord. In Jesus' Name, I pray. Amen.*

She suddenly understood that God spoke in a whisper, and if she was going to hear Him, she needed to be still and listen. Her entire Christian walk had been based on what she could accomplish through God instead of what God could accomplish through her.

"You just gonna sit around here in one of your trances, waiting for opportunity to knock?" Gladys came out onto the porch.

"No, Mom, I'm going back home to find work. God's given me a peace about you and Dad handling your recovery alone. I'll leave tomorrow, but I'll be here if you need me. You just call anytime, okay?"

"Stefani Mary Lucia Lencioni—"

Stefani walked toward her, enveloping her in a hug. The older woman stiffened and cringed under the closeness. As Stefani held her mother, she praised God for His miraculous healing. Knowing if her mother was going to be saved, it was going to be God's doing, not Stefani's. "I love you, Mom. God will be with you. If you get scared, you look in the Bible I gave you. Read the Psalms; He will give you peace."

"Ahh!" Gladys tossed her hand again.

sixteen

Stefani's eyes were wide with anticipation when she returned to the duplex. She came around the last corner muttering a prayer, hoping John would have returned home by now and they might work things out. She wanted to share with him all that God had taught her and how wrong she'd been. John was right about her stupid pride and inane financial goals and she couldn't wait to tell him so—and to humble herself as God had told her to do.

As their model Mediterranean home came into view, Stefani's shoulders slumped at the sight of several newspapers on John's doorstep. "John, please come home. I don't care if I have a future with you; I just want peace between us. I want to tell you I'm sorry for my pride and my arrogance," she said to the air.

Stefani unlocked her door and went directly to the answering machine, hoping her job search had proved more successful than her love life. By now, there should at least be a request for a job interview or two. She tossed her keys on the desk with a jingle and sat down, fighting disappointment when she noticed there were no messages at all. No job opportunities and no phone calls from John.

The afternoon sun filtered into her kitchen when a reflection shimmered across the wall. Stefani flew to the flowerbox window and saw John's SUV pull into the driveway. Tears welled up in her eyes at the sight of him and she flew to the front door.

Just as she leaped from her threshold, she noticed the elegant blond beside him. The woman was almost as tall as John and her long, slender legs were tucked neatly into svelte jeans and cowboy boots. Her blond hair seemed to glisten in the afternoon sunlight that peeked through the trees, and her fresh complexion was porcelain in nature.

Stefani knew getting caught up in idle jealousy would serve no purpose. Being humble before John and admitting her love for him would never be easy, but if she had any shot at a life with him, it would be necessary. "I'm trusting in my own power again, Lord. Give me the strength."

Stefani ran upstairs and grabbed her cowboy boots. She wriggled into her jeans and pulled her boots on. She let her hair fall loosely, running her fingers through it to emphasize its fullness. She puckered her lips and applied lipstick, hoping the subtle color would give her the confidence she needed. She emerged from her house just in time to see John's taillights turning the corner. Her heart sank.

She mustered up all her courage, muttering a continuous prayer, and drove up to the stables, following John's car at a careful, unseen distance. He pulled into the stable parking lot and helped the stunning blond from the passenger seat. Stefani parked behind a tree and sucked in a deep breath. She looked to the heavens for support. "It's now or never, Lord. Give me the strength. He has to know how I feel. Even if he doesn't return the feelings and even if there's someone else. I owe it to him to say how I really felt all those times I kept my mouth quiet when I should have said I loved him."

The California autumn was well under way, but it was still sunny and the ground was moist from the previous day's rain. It was chilly under the canopy of trees flanking the muddy roads, and she shivered as she emerged from her little coupe. She sloshed her way through the mud and into the stables. To her chagrin, John and the blond had disappeared. Stefani stopped in the doorway and noticed the young female rider from their night at the rodeo. She was brushing Kayla's mane.

"Hi," the young woman called before Stefani could retreat. She pulled the brush away from the horse and pointed it at Stefani. "You're John's friend, right? The one he brought to the rodeo that night."

"Uh—yes. Right," Stefani stammered.

"I knew he liked brunettes." She smiled and went back to brushing the horse.

Although the comment was meant as a compliment, the sting of jealousy touched Stefani. Seeing John with a blond that morning only compounded her pain. There were certainly no shortages of beautiful women in John's life. This young rider had long, flowing hair and sparkling, glacier blue eyes. Her face was perfectly proportioned and she could have easily been a fashion model. Stefani hadn't realized just how gorgeous Kayla's rider was under the cowboy hat and rodeo dust. Self-doubt plagued Stefani and she could think of no response. John now felt further away than ever. This woman only served as a vivid reminder that she'd blown it.

The blond spoke in her perky, schoolgirlish way. "I'm going to take Kayla out. You want to ride the ridge with me? The new horse is here and you'd save me another ride if you'd exercise her with me. I heard you've gotten pretty good on a horse."

Stefani tried to put aside her jealousy and focus on why she was here. If she really wanted to humble herself before John, she had to support him if he'd moved on. His young rider obviously supported him regarding Stefani. "Sure, a ride would be nice. Maybe you can show me a few moves," Stefani suggested. "I was really impressed with your riding that night at the rodeo."

"I was terrible that night. I didn't even get a score! But sure, I could show you a few moves. John's new horse is fabulous. Fully trained. You should see how tightly she cuts, and boy, is she gentle. Like an old stable mare tucked in the body of a rodeo champion. This way you can tell Uncle John personally that his horses were exercised. I don't want him to think Kayla or this new one were neglected while he was gone. I don't think Uncle John quite trusts anyone else with his horses. Even if I did grow up around them."

"*Uncle* John?"

"Uh-huh, he's my mom's brother," she continued casually. "Didn't he tell you that?" she asked innocently. "Usually, he tells people right away so they don't think he's dating some young girl. He gets embarrassed to be seen with me. Go figure. He doesn't look all that old to me and I say, let people think what they want."

"Uh, no, he failed to mention you were his niece."

"Probably because he was too concerned with my riding that night at the rodeo. He was right, though; it's always better to slow it down just a hair and go for the score than to knock a barrel down and lose any hope of winning by being disqualified. I'll be ready next time, though. It's so hard to fight the adrenaline when you're out there under the lights."

"John had mentioned he had a niece close by, but I never put the two together. He always calls *you* the trainer."

"That's because when it comes to the rodeo, your beau is all business," she laughed. "Winning is everything!" She lowered her voice and laughed. "He has no time for family connections. Oh, yeah, your beau has rodeo in his veins. He lives, eats, and breathes it, even living in the city."

"John's my landlord, not my beau," Stefani corrected.

"Uh-huh," she replied. "What's wrong with Uncle John, anyway? He's downright attentive, if I do say so myself. *When* you can get his mind off the rodeo or him saving us from the evil polluters."

"Nothing's wrong with John, I just didn't want you to get the wrong impression, that's all," Stefani explained.

"John said you went to Stanford. That's why I'm here; I just transferred for my junior year, much to my mom's dismay. My mother didn't want me coming out to *dangerous* California by myself. She thinks all you people do out here is drive by and shoot." She let out a small laugh. "Uncle John had mercy on me. He told my mom he'd take a transfer he'd been offered out here and keep an eye on me."

"That was sweet of him."

"Of course, Mom doesn't know about my barrel racing, but what does she expect when she hands me over to a former bull rider?" She laughed aloud.

"I'm sorry I don't remember your name," Stefani said.

"Justine Meadows."

"Well, I guess it's just us gals today, Justine. I'm Stefani." Stefani threw a saddle over the beautiful new animal and patted the horse on her nose, hoping they'd be long gone before John returned to the stables. Stefani was looking forward to the ride and the chance to escape her apology to John for the moment. "So what do you think of Stanford?"

"It's great. Met the man of my dreams there. Trevor Dane. We're going to be married at the end of the school year."

"Oh," Stefani said wistfully. "It must be nice knowing your future at such a young age." They started up the ridge. They were barely on the trail when a deep voice resonated through the quiet.

"Stefani! Stefani, wait!" It was John. Stefani turned to see him running toward her, the stunning other blond beside him, waving at her.

The sight of him reminded her how completely unprepared she was to meet him. Without thinking, she bolted on the horse. "Yah!" Stefani kicked the horse's hindquarters and sped up the path toward the ridge. Stefani was barely out of sight when she realized how much harder it would be to see John after running away. *Why am I acting so stupid? Why couldn't I have just pretended to be happy for John—even if he'd brought some cowgirl home with him?*

Stefani finally felt the full weight of John's new attachment. Her tears flowed freely and she sobbed aloud, knowing only the grazing cows and squirrels could hear. Even with God's help she wasn't strong enough to face John. . .to humble herself before another woman. She clung to Justine's words. *Your beau. . . Your beau. . .*When Stefani reached the top of the ridge, she slowed the horse to a mere trot. There was no going back now. Humiliation had won over humility.

She couldn't face him or his stunning new girlfriend. Stefani knew she paled in comparison to the lanky blond on John's arm.

She lifted her voice in prayer, "What now, Lord? What now?"

It wasn't long before she heard the galloping horse behind her and saw John quickly approaching on his horse, Kayla. Stefani was mortified. "Yah!" she sped up again and cut sharply up the hill to get away from him, but he was gaining on her. "Yah! Yah!" she yelled between frantic cries.

John appeared next to her, galloping at full speed. "Stop the horse, Stefani!" he yelled.

"NO!" she tried an even sharper cut she'd watched Justine perform at the rodeo, only to have the agile horse take her command too quickly for Stefani's apprentice riding skills. The horse turned on its tail and the last thing Stefani remembered was hurling through the air toward the muddy green pasture. When she came to, John was hovering over her, his deep green eyes thinned in concern.

"Stefani?" he asked softly.

"Justine taught me a few moves," she laughed aloud and then groaned in pain.

"You may want to practice them a few more times." He grinned, his wide smile baring his perfectly formed teeth and creating the tiny lines beside his eyes. He winked and she groaned again. "Stay still. Let's see whether anything's broken. Try moving one limb at a time, slowly," he urged. He watched as she carefully flexed one leg, then the other, then her wrists and elbows. "You fall very well. Gracefully, even; I was very impressed. Maybe barrel racing isn't your sport, but the bucking bronco might be."

"Is this supposed to make me feel better?" Stefani looked at the horse standing nearby grazing. "Look at her, she can't imagine why someone so incompetent would be riding her. She's mocking me!"

"They do that. You should see the bulls after they've just

kicked you off. They're worse than the horses. I think the bulls actually laugh. I think I even heard one say, 'Take that, you loser,' once."

Stefani laughed again and reached for her side to ease the pain. "This is why I'm a city girl," she moaned aloud. "Now I'm positive that saddles should have seat belts." She tried to get up, but her stomach lurched and the world tilted so she headed back toward flat ground.

"I don't know any city girl that rides a registered buckskin quarter horse and wears real cowgirl boots. You're a country girl; when are you going to admit it?" His eyes smiled again. He pressed above her abdomen and she screeched in pain. "I think you may have broken a rib or two." He clicked his tongue. "That's painful."

"Tell me something I don't know."

"Do you know I love you?"

"You love me? What about all those things I said to you about Atlas Semiconductors? You're not still angry with me?"

"How could I stay angry at the woman I love? Stubborn as she is. I'm just as stubborn, you know. But I suppose I'll have to prove that."

She grinned, but her smile disappeared as John bent down over her. She felt his warm breath upon her cheek and then she was lost in his gentle kiss. She felt his hand caress her chin and she lifted her head higher to get closer to him. His scent was like a warm, wonderful memory that washed over her powerfully. All her fears and anger dissipated within the strength of his kiss. There was a genuine honesty about it that left little room for doubt about his true nature. "Who's that beautiful blond you brought with you? You know, the one I just made a fool of myself over."

"So *that's* what your little chase was all about? Good, I was beginning to think I was in *real* trouble." He winked at her.

"Are you avoiding my question?" She tried to brush some of the mud from her jeans, but a thin layer was dried and caked on. The back of her arm was also covered in mud and she realized what a sight she must have been. She gingerly rose to her knees, but any farther proved impossible because of her sore ribs. Stefani whimpered and remained on her knees.

John knelt before her and wiped the mud from her hand before he took it. "Stefani, I do love you. I think I have from the moment you took me to that place with the mechanical bull and thought you were so funny," he laughed. "I know keeping my occupation a secret was wrong, but everything else I've done has been aboveboard. Scout's honor." He held up two fingers. "Will you believe me when I say you can trust me? What is it you want from me to prove that I am who I say I am?"

Stefani realized just how much damage her grandmother had unwittingly passed on when she heard the pain in John's voice. She had been raised to mistrust men. And she did. She had even questioned her own loving father. She believed he'd lost the farm, when it clearly made sense for her aging parents to sell the orchard to pay for her college expenses and begin their retirement. It was time to change—time to allow God to lead her. It was time to be loved and feel all that it offered: both the pain and extreme joy.

"John, I have been so unfair to you. You've given me every reason to trust you, but I *chose* to look at the one area that was questionable. And I never wanted an explanation about your job. I was afraid of what you might tell me. It's such a long story, but I was so wrong about workingmen."

"It was stupid to deceive you. I just didn't know how to tell you I was an EPA scientist. At first I was a little insulted by your attitude; I guess I just wanted you to admit you were attracted to a simple cowboy. I knew you felt the electricity in the room when we met that day in the duplex. It was undeniable. I wanted to prove to you that you could fall for a lowly cowboy, I guess to humble you. But then my feelings got in the way and I wanted so much more from you. I wanted you to fall in love with *me*—not a job title or a bunch of credentials, but *me*. It became harder and then too risky to tell you the truth as I got closer to shutting down Atlas. I didn't want you to know how I had deceived you. And I didn't want you in any danger. I just didn't have any choice."

"I know that now, John. And, yes, I did fall in love with the cowboy. It's *you* I love. The man who charmed my mother and showed me that being vulnerable is part of being loved. . . The man who taught me how to ride a horse and kissed me with a fire I've never known. . . *That* kiss had nothing to do with your education. *Unless* you majored in chemistry," she added and smiled.

Gentle lines appeared next to John's eyes as he softly brushed the wisps of hair from her face. He let out a low growl and kissed her again. "*We* major in chemistry, Miss Willems. Now, before I get caught up in this moment, are you ready to meet my sister?"

"Your sister? That's who the blond is? Oh," Stefani groaned, "I feel like such an idiot. I can't go meet her. Not now. She'll think I'm such a loon, taking off on your horse like that."

"She has her own drama to worry about." He kissed Stefani's forehead and stood. "How's your side? Can you get up?" He lifted her gingerly to her feet and she stood below him, locked in a loose, careful embrace. His wide, solid chest made up her entire view and she clung to his steady warmth.

"Ahem. We better go."

"I'm sorry about your job."

She reached up and pressed a soft kiss to his warm lips. "What job?"

"That's my girl." He kissed her again. "Come meet my sister." He took her by both hands. "I want to show her the woman who's stolen my heart."

"Oh, John, she'll think I'm crazy, running off like that on the horse."

"You are crazy, Stefani. If you weren't, we would have nothing in common," he teased. "Well, you're going to have to meet her sometime. No time like the present. We'll just tell her you were excited to test-drive your engagement present."

"My engagement present?"

"The horse. I'm allowing you to name her, so we'll have to change her registration papers later. She's yours."

"You bought *me* a horse. That's where you went?"

"What kind of cowboy would I be if my wife didn't have a horse?"

"Wife? You certainly were sure of yourself when you left."

He dropped to his knee and held her hands in his own. "Stefani Lencioni Willems, would you do me the honor of becoming my wife?"

The words she'd dreamt of for countless nights fell like a tropical rain upon her. She never thought she'd actually hear them. Certainly not from a man who made her weak in the knees. John was everything she'd envisioned and everything her grandmother warned her about. She looked down at her boots and knew she'd been captured. Lifting her lashes, she locked eyes with the rugged cowboy who exemplified all she'd once feared for her future: passion, submission, and a fiery attraction that felt dangerous, even illegal. She just stared into his eyes for a long time, taking in their obvious love for her and reeling at the idea that somebody loved *her* that way. She had never felt more special. "Yes," she managed.

"Yes?"

"Absolutely. Although my grandmother told me to find an accountant," she joked.

"An accountant, huh? Not a former bull rider?"

"I think I would have remembered if she had told me that."

"Well, one day you'll just have to explain to Grandma that God wrapped your husband in a different package."

"He certainly did," Stefani lifted her eyebrows.

"Oh, before I forget, I'm going to have the contractors come as soon as possible and make our duplexes into one happy home. We'll knock down the walls, take out a kitchen, and put in a nursery or two. What do you think?"

"I don't care where we live as long as we're together."

"Stefani Lencioni Willems, you have made my life a living nightmare over that house. Now that it's finally yours, you're telling me you don't care?" His fists flew to his hips and he gave her a threatening stare. "Did I miss something?"

"It's a woman's prerogative to change her mind," she shrugged.

"Dare I ask what brought this on?"

"It's a long story. I promised my grandmother I'd get the land back again, but Mom said that she didn't want it. It seems my grandmother was a little dotty by the end and I was confused about my true heritage. So now it doesn't matter anymore," she shrugged again. "See, it's quite simple actually."

"Am I supposed to understand any of that?"

"No, you just need to know that I've finally made peace with God, and whatever He wills for us, I take happily. If it's the duplex, so be it."

"I was all prepared to make that house into your dream home."

"John, any house with you in it is my dream home. Whether it's on my family's old orchard or in Timbuktu. Come a little closer, cowboy."

"Anything you say, princess." John wrapped his arms around her carefully. She winced and John gently helped her mount Kayla before him. They rode back to the stables with the new horse trailing behind them and the dwindling sun in the distance.

When they returned to the stables and dismounted, John's sister and Justine were hugging. John walked ahead with the horses, but Stefani followed, anxious to get to the comfort of her car. Her broken ribs ached with every step.

John tethered the horses to the fence and went toward his sister. "Justine and Angela, I'd like you to meet my fiancée, Stefani. Stefani, these charming ladies are my sister, Angela, and her daughter, Justine."

Stefani smiled and hugged both blonds, but moaned from their touch. Her body ached from her fall.

epilogue

Stefani saw her beloved duplex in a whole new light. It felt strange. Like she was visited by an entirely new history, instead of the happy, created memories she had clung to for so long. Knowing her grandfather was an alcoholic and had abused his wife and children sent a shiver down her spine. So much more made sense now: her grandmother's unrelenting hatred for laziness, the constant pressure on Stefani to have her own money, and the old woman's unrealistic view of Stefani's father that had been etched in her mind. Stefani was ashamed that she had believed her grandmother without question.

Stefani had rediscovered herself by knowing the horrifying truth of the family's life on the orchards. How ironic that she'd worked so hard to purchase something for her mother that brought only sadness and bitter memories. God had shown her, in vivid color, the flaw of being self-reliant.

She cuddled next to the fire with a warm mug and waited for John. He'd been gone all day on errands. She prayed over the several job offers she had and she took great pleasure in the fact that Bob Travers' illegal dealings had come to an end. Although her former boss had threatened to sue her personally and keep her from working, he had found himself being sued personally by the Environmental Protection Agency and facing a long list of criminal charges.

Gladys had continued to get well and was reading her Bible, and while she was making no further commitments at the time, she often had Bert reading it to her. No doubt her skeptical mother needed her husband's guidance as well. She prayed that her future wedding would serve as an opportunity for her parents to hear that everyone is acceptable for redemption.

The doorbell rang and Stefani jumped to meet her fiancé. John filled the doorway with a huge bouquet of pink roses, her favorite, and held out a tiny black velvet box. "John? What did you do?"

"Open it."

She pulled him in by the fire and they stood beside its warmth. She looked at his green eyes, smiling in their excitement. She slowly opened the tiny box and a key fell into her lap. "You got me a key?" she asked, her confusion evident.

"It's the key to my heart."

She wondered if she should thank him for the charming token or pinch him for teasing her unmercifully. She liked his teasing so she opted for a sweet, dimpled response: "John, you're so old-fashioned."

"And it's also the key to this great little ranch up in the redwoods by Kayla's pasture. I want you to see it before we buy it. It's perfect for a family. A big family."

"How big?" she asked tentatively.

"Well, we already have two horses. We can go from there."

He reached into his breast pocket and pulled out a diamond solitaire ring. "Is this what you were expecting?"

"John!" She couldn't believe her eyes. "It's kinda big!"

"Just like you imagined it would be." He grinned. "My sister told me women like gaudy rings. Is it gaudy enough for you?"

"It's disgusting!" she teased. She slipped it on her finger and watched the fiery lights play off its incredible color.

"So when can I make you mine? Do I have to wait for a big wedding?"

"I'm Italian, of course you have to wait for a big wedding. We'll have to find out when my Uncle Vito is available to play the accordion; it will be great! The funky chicken on the accordion is a must for any decent Italian wedding," she teased and rewarded him with her dimpled smile.

"I can hardly wait," he said without inflection.

"I love you, John Savitch."

"It's about time you admitted that."

"It's way past time." She kissed her husband-to-be with genuine passion. The truth had finally set her free. God's truth.

"Do nothing out of selfish ambition or vain conceit, but in humility consider others better than yourselves" (Philippians 2:3).

A Letter To Our Readers

Dear Reader:

In order that we might better contribute to your reading enjoyment, we would appreciate your taking a few minutes to respond to the following questions. We welcome your comments and read each form and letter we receive. When completed, please return to the following:

Rebecca Germany, Fiction Editor
Heartsong Presents
PO Box 719
Uhrichsville, Ohio 44683

1. Did you enjoy reading *The Landlord Takes a Bride?*
   - ❑ Very much. I would like to see more books by this author!
   - ❑ Moderately

   I would have enjoyed it more if ________________

   ____

   ____

2. Are you a member of **Heartsong Presents**? Yes ❑ No ❑
   If no, where did you purchase this book?______________

   ____

3. How would you rate, on a scale from 1 (poor) to 5 (superior), the cover design?________________________________

4. On a scale from 1 (poor) to 10 (superior), please rate the following elements.

   _____ Heroine _____ Plot

   _____ Hero _____ Inspirational theme

   _____ Setting _____ Secondary characters

5. These characters were special because________________

____

____

6. How has this book inspired your life?________________

____

____

7. What settings would you like to see covered in future **Heartsong Presents** books?____________________

____

____

8. What are some inspirational themes you would like to see treated in future books?____________________

____

____

9. Would you be interested in reading other **Heartsong Presents** titles? Yes ❑ No ❑

10. Please check your age range:

❑ Under 18	❑ 18-24	❑ 25-34
❑ 35-45	❑ 46-55	❑ Over 55

11. How many hours per week do you read?________________

Name ________________________________

Occupation ____________________________

Address ______________________________

City ______________ State __________ Zip __________